KISS MY ASSASSIN

DAVE SINCLAIR

KISS MY ASSASSIN

You've never met a spy like this before!

When the Turkish ambassador crashes his car in central London, the incident launches an unforeseeable series of catastrophic events—and a naked body.

MI6 spy Charles Bishop flies headfirst into intrigue, gun battles and assassinations. He's on the hunt for a mysterious and powerful arms-dealing organisation named Kali—and they have him squarely in their sights.

Along the way he falls for a mysterious woman who may just be the death of him.

Fast-paced with whip-smart dialogue and twists at every turn, *Kiss My Assassin* is the very definition of unputdownable.

NOTE TO THE READER

Although the Bishop novels can be read in any order, the events described take place before those in the *Eva Destruction* novels.

Dedicated to Biskit.
A cat who just shed all over my goddamn keyboard.

PROLOGUE

The rear wheels of the Mercedes slid, and Mohamed fought the wheel to avoid crashing into a traffic island. He retained control, but only just. The rain-drenched streets of London were eerily empty at this hour. As the car sped through the deserted streets, Mohamed wiped the ever-building sweat from his brow and tried to calm his hyperventilating breaths.

He shouldn't be here. He should be at home, tucked in bed beside his wife. Instead, he raced dawn's rise to do the unthinkable. How had events spiralled so far out of control? Only hours before he'd been celebrating the triumph of his career. Now he was ruined. Dishonoured. A criminal.

Fighting for control of the vehicle, Mohamed took the turn onto The Mall at speed. The new-model Mercedes did its best to counter his erratic steering, but technology could only assist so much. The car fishtailed unsteadily before righting itself. He was driving too fast. He knew that. But he couldn't slow down, not with the cargo he had. Not with what was at stake.

Speeding through a red light at Whitehall, Mohamed

saw the towering Houses of Parliament and Big Ben loom before him. This country was so proud of their hallowed bastion of democracy. It stood immovable and regal. It was in stark contrast to what would happen if he were discovered. His own country would fall apart like a house of cards. He could not let that transpire.

Screeching onto Westminster Bridge, Mohamed did his best to quiet his panicked breathing. He told himself to focus. No matter what, he had to succeed. His world had been shattered, but he could salvage it—but only if he kept his head.

The sight of water calmed him. It reminded him of home. Of safety. It reminded him of a place far from here.

Gregory should have been asleep hours ago, but his co-worker, Justin, hadn't turned up for work—*the slack gamer bastard*. Good old reliable Gregory had been forced to pull a double shift, again.

Gregory was saving for a house deposit with his girl-friend, Aisha, so it wasn't all bad. But damn, he was as exhausted as an insomniac zombie.

His warm bed beckoned. Not long now. He doubted ten hours at the wheel of a garbage truck would be anyone's idea of a good time. If it was, they certainly weren't someone he wanted to hang with. You don't need that kind of mental in your life. Thinking of what consti-tuted a good time guided Gregory's sleep-deprived mind to Aisha again. Nothing would be finer than slipping into their bed right now.

With a start, Gregory shocked himself alert. He'd closed his eyes for a fraction of a second and tumbled into a microsleep. Blinking several times did nothing to ease the lethargy overwhelming him. Gregory realised he had to get off the road. He was dead at the wheel.

Turning the big truck towards Westminster Bridge, Gregory tried to work out how long his shift had left. As best he could make out, it was somewhere between half an hour and a week. He needed coffee.

Waiting at the lights to turn onto Westminster Bridge Road, Gregory willed his eyes to stay open. The city seemed so empty. A thin veneer of rainwater coated the road, reflecting the street lights. The rhythmic beat of the blinker echoed in the cabin, lulling his drowsy mind. As soon as the light turned green, he accelerated.

The car came out of nowhere.

It careened through the intersection, seemingly oblivious to the red light. Gregory stamped his foot on the brakes, but the garbage truck was too big and cumbersome to stop suddenly. The driver of the Mercedes slammed on the brakes too late, and the car spun. It kept bowling towards the truck.

Gregory closed his eyes and braced for impact.

PC Genevieve Williams heard the screech of tyres. She'd just finished her patrol along Queen's Walk and was about to make her way across the river to HQ when she heard it. It was never a pleasant sound. She instinctively waited for the howl of twisted metal.

The garbage truck had turned with the lights and proceeded into the intersection. The maniac in the Mercedes must have run the light. The driver realised too late and tried to stop, but it was useless.

The thud of metal on metal was horrific. The truck collided with the rear side panel of the Mercedes, sending it spiralling across the asphalt. The slick road only aided the car's chaotic spin. Chunks of plastic and metal were strewn in all directions, and the rear boot flew open as the car continued to whirl across the bridge.

The driver's side of the Mercedes hit the curb with such force its opposite wheels were thrust into the air. A flesh-coloured object was hurled from the boot. It sailed through the air for what seemed like hours, then hit the footpath with a wet, meaty slap and slid, coming to rest against the bridge railing.

After three years on the force, PC Williams was no rookie, but it took several seconds of post-collision silence for her mind to process what had just happened.

A garbage truck and an expensive luxury car had just crashed into one another, and in the process a completely naked body had been flung from the boot of the car and now lay motionless on Westminster Bridge.

Scrambling for her whistle, PC Williams blew frantically. The garbage truck was closest. She hoisted herself onto the running board and peered into the cabin.

"Are you alright, sir?"

The driver was dazed, his gaze unfocused. "Yeah, yeah I think so." His watery eyes turned to the crumpled car. "Check on them. Oh god."

Already moving, PC Williams ran to the driver's side of the Mercedes and yanked the door open. The driver was a middle-aged man with a Mediterranean complexion. He had a cut above his eye, but he was alive.

"Sir, are you okay?" Stunned silence was the only reply. "Sir, you've been in a traffic collision. Are you alright?"

Receiving no response, PC Williams left the car and approached the most worrying of persons involved. Lying on the wet footpath, illuminated by the city, the naked male body lay prone. He wasn't breathing. Genevieve suspected he hadn't for some time—possibly hours. In her few short years on the force, she'd seen her share of dead bodies. This one wasn't fresh. The pallid complexion told her that autolysis had already taken hold. The skin was loose, there were early signs of bloat. This person's death hadn't been caused by the crash. Something else was at play.

Grabbing her radio, PC Williams called it in. She had to secure the scene and needed every available officer. Dispatch assured her they would be there in minutes.

The driver of the Mercedes staggered from his car. Without looking in PC Williams' direction, he stumbled away from the crash site, heading down the long stretch of Westminster Bridge.

"Oi, you're under arrest, mate," Genevieve shouted. "Stay where you are."

The man continued to totter away, either oblivious to her warning, or ignoring it. She chased after him. Rounding on the dishevelled man, PC Williams halted his advance by shoving a palm into his shoulder.

"Sir, I'm arresting you for traffic violations and in connection to the dead body you were transporting in your vehicle. You do not have to say anything, but it may harm your defence if you do not mention—"

"Diplomatic immunity!" The man became animated, as if suddenly aware of his situation.

"What?"

"Diplomatic immunity!" He was practically shrieking. "You cannot arrest me. I am a diplomat. I am the Turkish ambassador to the United Kingdom. You cannot arrest me."

Genevieve shook her head. "That's a dead body, mate. You can't claim—"

"Diplomatic immunity!"

"Yeah, exactly. You can't claim that."

"What?" The man shook his head.

"What?"

The diplomat frowned in confusion. "What, what?"

Genevieve sighed. It was going to be a long night. "You're not going anywhere, sir, diplomatic immunity or not. Go stand over there."

The man realised the futility of refusal and complied. Genevieve called dispatch and asked to be connected to her superior.

"Guv, you might want to come down here. I, ah, I've got a bit of a situation."

"What kind of situation, Williams?"

"The headline kind." She looked at the prostrate body on the bridge. "You might want to start waking some people up."

CHAPTER ONE

"Who drives around with a body in their boot?" asked Paul Cavendish, Head Spec Ops at MI6.

"Idiots?" Bishop suggested helpfully. He watched his boss carefully. He was agitated, but there was something else at play.

"Well, idiots obviously," Paul replied, annoyed, "but more specifically, why would the Turkish ambassador be driving around at 4 am with a dead body in his boot?"

"Maybe he's a big *Weekend at Bernie's* fan?"

Paul glared at Bishop evenly. "Perhaps. Then again, perhaps you're due for a posting in Myanmar."

"Right you are, boss." Bishop nodded at his superior.

Paul's face broke into a familiar smile, which Bishop returned. He enjoyed his boss's humour. It was a fine way to start the day. The two sipped tea in Paul's office at Vauxhall Cross, discussing the early morning's events.

Every major, and quite a few minor, government departments had been thrown into a political shitstorm that social media had dubbed the "Body on the Bridge Incident". Bishop was less than impressed at the inventiveness of that one. So far the ambassador had remained tight-lipped, and the body hadn't been identified.

MI6 were involved purely from an intelligence standpoint. They had no authority to work within UK borders unless the State Secretary granted immunity under the Intelligence Services Act. Given the unknown state of affairs, that seemed unlikely. The best they could manage was relying on the good graces of other departments to keep them involved.

The ambassador's claim for diplomatic immunity was problematic. The whole thing was a political nightmare. Technically, City of London police could arrest him, as diplomatic immunity only extended so far, but they'd chosen not to, at least for now. He was being held without charge, but the clock was ticking. They could only hold him for twenty-four hours. If charges weren't laid, he'd be on the first plane out, and the whole thing would forever remain unsolved.

The likelihood of an official arrest increased as more and more politicians and experts were interviewed on morning TV programs. Bishop could see the pressure building. Soon there would be outright calls for the ambassador to be held accountable for whatever crime had been committed. In the interim, Metropolitan Police were in possession of an unidentified, but politically charged, corpse.

"So where do we come in?" Bishop asked.

As much as he enjoyed his chats with Paul, his boss never had a casual discussion without some sort of agenda. The fact that the topic of conversation was the Westminster Bridge incident meant Bishop was to be involved in some shape or form.

"This has international consequences, obviously," Paul raised his teacup. "Turkey's government is on a knife edge at the moment. Whatever this is may be used for leverage by foreign governments—or perhaps that's what caused it in the first place. Who knows? Regardless, we need answers." Paul looked up and raised an eyebrow. "And that's where you come in."

"Is it now?" Bishop folded one leg over the other. *Here we go*, he thought. "And how exactly would I come into it?"

"I've arranged for you to have a little tête-à-tête with the ambassador in question. Demir is his name."

Bishop realised he shouldn't have been surprised. As a domestic matter, this would fall within the purview of London Police; MI5 at a pinch, if it had international ramifications. MI6 would be far down on the list of agencies able to shove their weight around. There was no doubt Paul had pulled some strings to get Bishop a seat at the table.

"Where is he now?" he asked.

"Lambert Estate, just outside of Buckinghamshire."

"Fancy."

Paul nodded. "It was deemed too gauche to throw him in a local cell with Knuckles McGinty and Jimmy the Seat Sniffer."

"Positively progressive by the Met," Bishop observed. "Or were they afraid of reprisals?"

Paul pondered the question. "Probably a bit of both, to be honest. You'll have half an hour with him. This is purely ceremonial. No need to perform an interrogation like Kandahar."

"I still maintain he deliberately ran into my fist, the little bugger."

"Many times, if I recall correctly."

Bishop shrugged. "When do I leave, boss?"

"It's teed up for two hours from now, so you'd better get your skates on."

Bishop checked his watch. Buckinghamshire was

about an hour away. Readying himself to leave, Bishop examined his boss more closely. "You look a bit worse for wear, if you don't mind me saying."

"Why would a superior mind his subordinate telling him he looks dreadful?" Paul chuckled to show there was no malice, then sighed. "Nancy has a new friend. She invited her around for dinner last night and things got messy. My god, those Australians can drink. Lovely girl, but I foresee she's going to be trouble."

"Australian, hey? Can't say I've ever had an Australian girl."

"If last night is anything to go by, I highly recommend steering clear."

"I'll keep that in mind."

Paul tilted his head. "Never an Australian? That surprises me. I would have thought you'd have coloured in the map of the world with your countless conquests."

Doing his best to appear offended, Bishop held a splayed hand to his chest and, with the innocence of a choirboy, said, "I take umbrage to that, good sir!"

An eye roll was Paul's only response. Both men knew Bishop was no male vestal virgin. His skills with the opposite sex had been used many times to entice informants to supply critical information. They may have been traitors, but they were satisfied traitors. Using sex as a weapon wasn't something Bishop was especially proud of, but he had obtained indispensable intelligence for the United Kingdom. Besides, no one had been killed, and he always made sure the informer was well taken care of. In more ways than one.

He didn't need a therapist to tell him his proclivities had bled into his personal life. Unable to commit to more than a one-night stand, he was aware he had an abject fear of commitment. Not that he wasn't enjoying himself in the process. He was a young man. He had many seeds to sow before the idea of settling down even appeared on the horizon. Regardless, he knew it was something he would be forced to confront one day. He just hoped it wasn't soon.

The two men exchanged a hearty handshake and Bishop bid his superior farewell.

"And Charles," Paul said, seemingly as an afterthought, though Bishop had the feeling it was anything but. "Take care to ask the ambassador if there are any outside pressures MI6 could, let's say, assist with. Never a bad thing for His Majesty's government to be owed a favour by a representative of a foreign power." His features grew slightly darker. "It's purely a hunch, but I have an inkling this will have far greater implications than just one little ambassador's indiscretion."

"Will do, sir."

There it was. No matter how casually Paul had approached the subject, there were larger machinations at play. Bishop wouldn't be involved unless MI6 were worried. And if MI6 were worried, everyone should be.

The gravel driveway crunched under the tyres of Bishop's brand-new black Audi. The gardens of Lambert Estate were so cultivated and moulded they were almost unreal. Too well-shaped, too verdant. It was as if an American had dreamed up what they thought an English estate should look like. The outlying forest soon gave way to lush manicured lawns, which led to a quaint, picture-postcard manor. It was like a scene from the lid of a shortbread tin.

Bishop parked and walked slowly towards the manor.

He counted three armed police officers roaming the grounds, all wearing tactical vests over their crisp uniforms. Each carried Heckler & Koch MP5SFs. They weren't taking any chances.

Inside, he met with the lead protection officer, an officious woman by the name of Underwood. She was a stern sergeant who seemed immune to Bishop's charm. He liked her immediately. She led him to a delightful sun-drenched conservatory at the rear of the house.

The ambassador sat in a lounge chair, taking in the garden view while drinking what appeared to be an espresso. He seemed cosy, sipping away in a warm scarf. In the distance, by the far garden, a uniformed officer patrolled, a black bulletproof vest over his white shirt.

Underwood left with a curt nod.

"Good afternoon, Ambassador." Bishop offered his hand.

The ambassador didn't take his eyes off the garden panorama. "Where are you from? The department of sanitation and passive-aggressive parking signs?"

"MI6."

The ambassador turned, surprised. He sat up straight. His face said, *this is more like it.*

Though he was more alert, there was wariness in his eyes. He nodded for Bishop to sit. "So many people have come to ask me questions, I'm considering hiring myself out as a fortune teller."

Bishop gave him a friendly frown. "I'll give you a fiver if you can tell me who wins the four o'clock at Ascot."

"Jezebel's Revenge, but it's only three to one, hardly worth your time."

He was smart, Bishop surmised. And funny. Good, he could work with that.

The ambassador assessed him, from his expensive haircut to his Salvatore Ferragamo shoes. "Are you sure you're a spy? You look more like a catwalk model."

"Most definitely a spy, sir. My name is Bishop. It seems you're in a bit of a pickle."

Ambassador Demir raised an amused eyebrow. "You have a talent for understatement, Mr Bishop."

"One of many. You should see my karaoke."

"There's no need to try and captivate me with your charm." There was a hint of condescension in the ambassador's voice. "I am an ambassador, my role is to engage people on a personal level. I know how to win their trust, to find out what we can do for one another."

"It seems you have a greater need for my assistance than I do yours at the moment, if you don't mind me saying, Ambassador."

"Ooh, very good. Excellent. A reaffirmation of my dire situation with an offer of a lifeline. You have some experience in this, I see. It is a shame it will all be for nought, I'm afraid. But still, good going."

"And why would it be for nothing?"

The ambassador leaned forward and gave a cheerless grin. "Because I will soon be dead, Mr Bishop."

"Look, I know the food here is not what you're accustomed to…"

"No." The ambassador shook his head. "Perhaps you are less experienced than I thought. That was not the time for a humorous quip. We've moved past the initial amiable trust exercise, you've reinforced the lifeline, now this is where you offer to do your best to get me out of this mess." He tutted. "Perhaps I would have been better off with the department of sanitation and passive-aggressive parking signs."

Bishop could see why the ambassador had risen to

one of the most important postings his country had. He was shrewd, knew human behaviour, could negotiate unflinchingly and did it all while maintaining an affable persona. He was good. But Bishop had a counter to his years of diplomatic experience. The truth.

"Very well, let's speak plainly shall we, Ambassador Demir? To put it bluntly, you're fucked. You've been caught transporting a dead body in your own car. Your refusal to disclose who it is or how it got there means you'll be charged with murder. In such cases, diplomatic immunity means less than a warm cup of piss in hell. You're screwed, and no amount of arrogance is going to change that. Right now, I'm your only ally. I suggest you talk to me before I send in the real Department of Sanitation."

Bishop could see the cogs in the ambassador's brain whirling. His dire situation was not aided by his posturing. Surely he understood that? It was mere hours before he would be charged. Once that occurred, he'd be hauled into custody and humiliated before the press and his country. Perhaps his bravado was a last hurrah, the final act of a public servant before he was stripped of his status.

Then again, perhaps not.

There was something in Demir's manner that seemed at odds with a man at the end of his career, a man facing disgrace. There was a Zenlike calmness to him that went beyond acceptance. It was like the serenity of a death-row inmate consuming their final meal. There was more going on than Bishop realised. Time to find out what it was.

"Ambassador, perhaps before they clap the handcuffs on, you might want to tell me what's going on. I may be able to help."

A bitter laugh escaped Demir's lips, surprising them both. The ambassador explained. "I'm afraid no one can help me, Mr Bishop. My family, my wife, my children, they will also pay the price. But perhaps…" His eyes clouded over in contemplation. "Perhaps you could do something about those who have sealed my fate."

"Sealed your fate? I'm sorry, I don't understand."

The ambassador waved a dismissive hand. "I had a meeting. A secret meeting. Not officially sanctioned by my government, but, well, let's just say it was encouraged, yes? This meeting, it would not strictly be against UN guidelines, but it would certainly be viewed as," he tilted his head, "distasteful. It was with a trader, a merchant of ordnances. He was the man discovered on the bridge."

"He was an arms dealer?"

"Among other things." Demir leaned forward, as if suddenly aware that others could be listening. "We were not trading arms last night, no money was exchanged, nothing of the sort. In fact, we were celebrating."

"What were you celebrating, Ambassador?"

A bitter cackle. "The highlight of my career, or so I thought. I'd successfully parleyed a seat at the table. I'd honestly thought there was every chance we would miss out, but I negotiated hard, used every trick I knew, and we got in. I was elated. We had prepared for this for months and it had paid off. I suggested we celebrate, and he agreed. I was giddy as a schoolgirl, as the saying goes." Despite the positive words, the ambassador's demeanour remained sour.

"But something went wrong?"

Demir nodded. "At my behest, we moved to a Turkish bath, to celebrate, yes? As is the way of things, we drank, we ate, but appetites were not, shall we say, sated." His expression turned grim. "We engaged the services of a prostitute." The ambassador's eyes drifted to the garden in the distance. "Things became… enthusiastic, out of hand. In the commotion, the dealer slipped." The ambassador turned to Bishop, his eyes pleading. "Please believe me, it was an accident. A tragic, unfortunate accident. I shared no hatred with this man. In fact, he had supplied the means to help my country a great deal. It was a mishap, one that ended tragically."

"That's why he was naked? The arms dealer in your boot?"

Again, Demir bobbed his head.

"The girl, where is she?" Bishop asked.

Confusion crinkled the ambassador's face. "What girl?"

"My apologies for the clichéd assumption." Bishop cleared his throat. "The prostitute."

"He will remain quiet. He can be trusted. If he survives at all."

Ignoring that ominous statement for now, Bishop pressed on. "Why didn't you just contact the dealer's employer and advise of the terrible accident?"

"You don't know these people!" Demir bellowed, suddenly agitated. "There is no such thing as 'accidents'. There are no mistakes. You can't seek mercy from these people."

"But you're the client. It's you who gives them the money for goods. Why would you be afraid of that? How can they have so much power that—"

"They hold all the power!" Taking a moment to calm himself, the ambassador went on. "We realised this long ago. These are not mere merchants, selling us a box of cheap Chinese pistols. If you say no, or do not purchase the volume they offer, they will supply the other side twice as much, and you will pay in blood and death. I represent my country, Mr Bishop. You find my dealings with these people unsavoury, I can see it in your eyes. I do not care for your condescension. But these people, you do not trifle with. They will come after your entire family, your friends. They will slice open the throats of every single person you love until they get what want. You ask how I can be afraid? I will tell you. Once you cross paths with these people you will do as they say until your death. Kuolema can snap his fingers and you are dead. That is why I am talking to you now. I will be dead within the day. My family, dead. Everyone I know, everyone I love, dead."

"That's a lot of death."

"You mock me? You think I exaggerate, Mr Bishop? You think I revel in the fact that everyone I care most about in this world will soon be dead? I just want it over."

The ambassador became more agitated as he went on. The reaction seemed genuine, but for the life of him, Bishop couldn't comprehend anyone who could instil such fear. Certainly not someone he'd never heard of.

Bishop did his best to appear sympathetic. "If this will happen as you say, why not warn them, put them under protection?"

"Kuolema does not care about protection. He cares not for anything that stands in his way. I represent my country. I am esteemed among my peers. I hold power, the ability to influence my government and others around the world. That is nothing. Nothing at all. Not to these people. Theirs is a world of shadow, a splinter of an idea. They are wraiths, Mr Bishop. How do you catch a wraith, a ghost? You can't."

"That's very dramatic."

"As is death. We have a saying in Turkey, Mr Bishop. *Ne ekersen, onu bicersin.* One who sows wind will reap hurricanes. With all the resources you no doubt have, I caution you not to cross these people unless you are certain. In all likelihood you will lose.

Your family will lose. Those you care for most in the world will lose."

"I'll keep that in mind." Fortunately, there were very few people Bishop cared for, and even less who cared for him. "Who is this Kuolema?"

"No one knows. He is the head of the organisation, or so it is thought. We sent three of our spies to find out if he really existed. None returned."

"What were you buying? The thing you were celebrating in the bathhouse?"

"An invitation."

"To?"

"An auction, Mr Bishop. An auction. I was to leave the day after tomorrow. The auction is only four days from now; we were cutting it fine. That is what we celebrated, my enrolment in the auction."

"And where is this auction?"

"Marrakech."

"In Morocco?"

"No, the Marrakech just outside Liverpool. Of course Morocco." The ambassador scowled, but went on. "The auction is run by a Mr Temple. A Frenchman with a villa there, I believe."

Far in the distance, Bishop heard the distinct pop of gunfire. It was far away, but its presence was alarming. He doubted the security detail would be undergoing target practice with a subject so close. He heard shuffling in the house. Others had noticed too.

More gunfire sounded, now accompanied by urgent shouts. It grew louder.

"What's that?" Bishop asked, more to himself than to Demir.

"Consequences, Mr Bishop. Consequences. Kali is here."

"The goddess? I should have shaved and put on a clean shirt."

Demir ignored the quip. "I don't fear god, little man. I fear them."

"I don't understand."

"Kali is an organisation. Kuolema is the head of Kali."

"An arms-dealing organisation named after a multi-armed deity? Someone overdosed on irony."

More gunfire could be heard; it grew louder. Guards rushed about, confusion smacked across their faces. Bishop could read their thoughts. How had a routine babysitting assignment gone to hell so suddenly?

Underwood rushed into the room, pistol out, face red. "The control room's gone dead. Officers aren't answering their hails. We're under attack."

"We need to get him out of here." Bishop nodded towards the ambassador.

"No, we need to protect him, not take him out in the open." Underwood's face was calm, but a tremor in her voice betrayed the fact that she was rattled.

Arguing wasn't going to help, but Bishop knew he had a better chance of saving the ambassador if they moved now. Unfortunately, he wasn't the one in charge.

In contrast to Underwood's quiet anxiety, Demir projected a serene pretence of being at peace with the world. He glanced at the MI6 agent and shrugged. "Consequences, Mr Bishop. I suggest you make peace with whatever divine being you choose. You shall be meeting them very soon."

Bishop scanned outside. As if on cue, the police officer by the far garden fell forward. He didn't move again.

Underwood saw it too. "Shit! We're down to three. We need to—"

Officer Underwood's words were cut short by a smash of glass. A red welt appeared in the centre of her forehead as the back of her skull was blown out. She collapsed in a silent pile on the plush carpet.

Demir's Zenlike calm shattered as he leapt out of his chair. Grasping the back of his head, Bishop forced the diplomat unceremoniously to the floor behind the couch, where they offered no direct line of sight to wherever the sniper was positioned.

"Stay down." Rolling over to Underwood's corpse, Bishop took her pistol and tucked it into the back of his pants. He figured he'd need the additional rounds. "If this is your Kali friends, Ambassador, they're very good at what they do." Bishop counted the rounds and checked the two exits to the room.

"My god, man!" the ambassador cried. "That woman was just killed in front of you. Do you not care?"

Demir had certainly broken loose from his calm acceptance of only moments before. The act had never fooled Bishop.

"She was a professional. She would want me to perform my duty and protect her charge. And that's what I intend to do…" Bishop yanked Demir's head down as he moved to peer over the back of the couch. "Provided he does everything I say."

"It won't make a difference, you know. Kali will kill us both."

"Well, see, I'll have to disagree with you there." Bishop pulled back the hammer of the pistol. It was purely for effect. "I'm in a god-killing kind of mood."

Taking a moment to close his eyes, Bishop ran through the logistics. He recalled the configuration of the manor he'd passed through, the distance to his car, which pocket contained the keys, the number of bullets in both guns, and what objects could be used as weapons when the bullets ran out. Everything else was chance.

"Why—" The ambassador recoiled from the spy. "Why on earth are you smiling, man?"

Not aware that he had been, Bishop ignored the question. "Stay behind me. Don't pause, don't dally. You do, you're dead. Don't get too close, I need to be able to move freely when we encounter trouble. You do, you're dead. If I tell you to do something, either you do it that second—"

"Or I'm dead?" the ambassador asked with disdain.

"You're a smart man. Let's go."

CHAPTER TWO

Crouching low, Bishop and the ambassador made for the door that Underwood had come through. Ducking behind furniture, they avoided any clear line of sight from the garden. Their pace was careful but rapid; the longer they took, the better position their enemy would be in. And Bishop wasn't about to supply any advantage to an adversary.

Reaching the back of the open door, he held up a hand to halt the ambassador. Demir walked straight into his palm. Bishop shot him an irritated look and shook his head. He opened his eyes wide, as if to say, *pay attention*.

From the hallway came the soft patter of footsteps. Looking the ambassador up and down, Bishop leaned over and removed his scarf. Demir opened his mouth but remained silent. From a nearby coffee table Bishop picked up a pencil. The ambassador regarded him as if he were mad, but Bishop held a finger to his lips as he watched a shadow pass the crack of the open door.

It didn't take long. The barrel of the submachine gun came through first. Bishop waited agonising seconds until the rest of the weapon appeared, its holder cautious. Wise. But not wise enough.

Bishop grasped the hand guard of the gun, thrusting the barrel upwards. With his other hand he shoved the pencil behind the trigger and flicked the safety on. The would-be assassin grunted and came into view. Bulky build, three-day growth and a series of scars across his face. Thug personified.

The thug fought to gain control of the weapon, trying to wrestle it free from Bishop's grasp. The MI6 agent released his grip, and the thug rattled the gun in frustration as it refused to fire. Bishop looped the ambassador's scarf around his pistol until it was fully enclosed, then gripped the thug's head and raised the pistol to his neck. He fired once.

The muffled shot severed the thug's spinal column and his life. He dropped to the ground limply. Bishop unfurled the scarf and offered the impromptu silencer to the ambassador, who stared wide-eyed and slowly shook his head.

Dropping the scarf to the floor, Bishop jerked his head, indicating for Demir to follow. He had no idea how many obstacles stood between them and freedom. At a guess, there had to be at least six, given they were able to take out four unsuspecting police. Possibly more. He'd held the element of surprise over his first victim, but that wouldn't last. They had to move.

Carefully stepping into the hallway, Bishop swept the area with his gun. Clear. He nodded his head, and Demir followed. Both men trod carefully.

The hallway was too open, with long stretches of no cover. They had to move quickly, but that meant making more noise. It was a balancing game.

Given time, Bishop would have admired the ornate

Georgian hallway. But that wasn't on his mind just then. Survival was.

At the halfway point they passed a hallway stand. Without missing a step, Bishop picked up a bright green decorative glass bauble, slipped it into his pocket and kept moving. The ambassador gave the MI6 agent an odd look but said nothing.

Ahead, Bishop heard the slow, measured creak of a door opening. The police would never be so careful, so Bishop could only surmise it was an unfriendly arrival. He forced his tense body to unfurl. He had to be loose. He had to be ready.

Yanking Demir by the collar, he pulled him into the nearest room. It turned out to be a library. No additional weapons in here, unless they intended to bore the Kali to death with Kierkegaard.

On the opposite side of the hall was a door to what seemed like a parlour of some sort. Extracting the ornamental bauble from his pocket, Bishop crouched into a baseball pitcher's stance. Demir's mouth dropped open. He seemed to believe Bishop had finally slipped into madness.

Throwing the pitch across the hallway, the bauble found a hard surface in the parlour and smashed with an unholy *crash*. With the ambassador crouched behind a desk, Bishop found a dark corner with a direct line of fire across the hall. Pistol raised, he took an upright Weaver stance and waited. Agonising seconds ticked away.

The footsteps in the hallway were cautious. Bishop heard faint rustles of fabric; probably the sound of hand gestures indicating what would happen next.

They were trained and patient. So was Bishop.

The first intruder slithered up to the parlour doorway, KRISS Vector submachine gun pointed skyward. That was some serious hardware for one little ambassador.

Moments later his compatriot joined him, issuing a reassuring nod. Turning to face the wall, they readied themselves to pounce.

The two had less facial scarring than the previous intruder Bishop had encountered. All had hard faces, like ex-military. Fair complexions, but deeply tanned, like they'd seen a lot of sun over extended periods.

They were about to burst in, all guns firing. Too aggressive and prone to high casualties for Bishop's liking. Aware they could move at any second, he acted.

The first shot took out the intruder closest to the door, destroying the back of his head. A second quick tap through the centre of his back guaranteed the kill. The second intruder had time to react and swung around to face Bishop, shocked smeared across his features.

The movement meant Bishop's headshot missed its mark. Instead of a clean centre of the forehead round, it entered his cheek, dislodging his jaw in an agonising injury. He screamed in pain, clutching his severed body part. A further bullet to his heart ended the agony.

The element of surprise was now blown. Anyone around the house would have heard the shots and come running. They had to move. No time to search the bodies, no time to untangle the weapons strapped underneath them.

With a flick of his thumb, Bishop motioned for the ambassador to follow. They entered the hallway on high alert, searching for further threats.

As Demir stepped over the prone corpses, he whispered, "That was not honourable, Mr Bishop."

"Perhaps an honourable man would care." Bishop observed both ends of the hall. "I wouldn't know."

No point in being stealthy anymore, the two men charged down the hallway towards the front entrance. Bishop updated his mental calculations. He'd taken down three. There were anywhere from one to ten more obstacles before them. He hoped for the former.

Nearing the grand entrance, Bishop's eye caught a shadow that fell across the front window. Another intruder held his KRISS submachine gun as he swivelled his head towards the garden, watching for threats. He was looking the wrong way. A carefully timed bullet through the window crumpled his now-lifeless body.

Bishop whispered, "It's glass. Who uses glass for cover? I have to wonder who trained these people—Helen Keller?"

The ambassador wisely chose not to answer. They were at the front door. It was now a game of odds. With four down, their chances were improving, but there was no way of telling if the odds were in their favour. There was only one way to find out.

Bishop flung the door open and counted to six. He stepped out, pistol at the ready. Having taken down the front of house guard, they were fortunate, but it wouldn't hold. The ambassador followed Bishop's shadow and they slowly made their way across the portico, scanning for foes.

The fallen intruder by the window lay sprawled on the garden bed, his submachine gun glistening in the sun. Bishop had counted his bullets; his pistol was out.

He turned to the ambassador. "Do you know how to fire a gun?"

"I have seen it in the movies."

"I've seen tap dancing in the movies, that doesn't make me Fred Astaire. I'll take that as a no."

Before they could reach the machine gun, a huge shadow fell across the garden. From around the corner of the building a massive hulk of a man stomped towards them. The other intruders had been well-muscled, but this guy was something else. Angry disposition and arms like felled trees, he looked like he crushed skulls in his spare time.

Demir stepped back from the approaching behemoth. "Good lord."

The giant of a man aimed his own submachine gun at them. The pistol in Bishop's hand was empty, and he couldn't reach the dead guard's machine gun without being cut down. Bishop held up his hands and took his finger from the pistol's trigger.

Sizing up the intruder, Bishop smirked. He tossed his pistol aside and raised his fists in a boxing stance. "Let's settle this like men, shall we?"

The man-mountain grinned.

The ambassador's mouth flapped open. "Are you mad? Look at the size of him!"

The man-mountain placed his submachine gun on the grass. He stood tall and cracked his neck, limbering up.

The MI6 spy shook his head. "Lunatic."

Bishop reached around and extracted Underwood's pistol from the back of his pants. The man-mountain's mouth gaped open and he lunged for his weapon. Too late. Bishop landed three shots in quick succession, one head, two chest. Each found their mark, and the huge man collapsed onto the grass, dead eyes open.

"That's for Underwood." Turning to Demir, Bishop said, "Let's go."

They jogged towards Bishop's car.

Between panting breaths, Demir grimaced. "Like I said, not honourable, Mr Bishop."

"Do me a favour when we're driving out of here? Check your pulse. If you still have one I'd kindly ask you to shut it, thank you, Mr Ambassador."

Unsure if he had terminated the last of the intruders, Bishop took no chances. They took a weaving course towards the Audi, ensuring no one could get a clean shot. Keys in hand, he unlocked the car and they were in.

Before the ambassador had time to put his seatbelt on Bishop started the car and took off. The ambassador was flung against his door. Zipping down the gravel driveway, Bishop thought of relaxing, but it was too soon. First he had to get the ambassador to safety.

Who were these goons? Who the hell had the balls to murder police in broad daylight? Was it the mysterious Kali arms dealers Demir had spoken of? They must think they're untouchable if they thought they could kill police and ambassadors without consequence. No foreign government would ever be so provocative. It would be considered an act of war.

Perhaps it was.

Safety first. Then questions. Vengeance soon after.

Reaching the end of the driveway of Lambert Estate, Bishop prepared to swing the powerful car onto the road. The polite use of an indicator seemed inappropriate, given the circumstances.

The sound was deceptively small, like the plop of a dropped egg. But the spray of blood across the windscreen told Bishop the ambassador had been shot. Mid-turn, Bishop lost control of the vehicle. The Audi's wheels slid out on the gravel and when they hit asphalt, the car went sideways.

The world tumbled before Bishop's eyes. Flipping violently across the road, the car crunched and flew apart as it rolled three times before smashing into the far embankment, upside down.

The interior of the overturned car was all airbags, flying glass, powder and pain. Blood flooded Bishop's vision. His own, he guessed, but he had no idea from where. Agony consumed him, but he didn't know the source of that either.

Beside him, the ambassador's lifeless eyes stared blankly into some unknown void.

Bishop's vision was blurred, like he'd put on someone else's prescription glasses. He fought the oncoming blackout. He lost.

The world went dark.

Blurred vision returned. How long had he been out? A second? An hour?

Outside, all Bishop could see was the driveway he'd just left.

He coughed blood. It gurgled in his upside-down throat.

Blackness.

Then Bishop saw the bottom half of a figure striding down the driveway.

Blackness.

He snapped to consciousness. The figure was close now, across the road. He could see their full height. The figure stood tall, grey hood over their head, face obscured. In their hands, a sniper rifle.

Bishop struggled with the seatbelt above him, his hands slick with blood, unable to release him from his inverse position.

Blackness.

With his last remnant of strength, Bishop's bloody hand reached for the belt release, his fingers like spaghetti. Shades of black stabbed into his vision. His fingers refused to work. His unfocused eyes could see the hooded figure taking aim. There were shouts. Tyres skidded. Bishop coughed blood.

Everything went black.

The chirp of birds woke him.

He lay beneath crisp white sheets in a crisp white room. Hospital.

Planting his fists on the bed, he pushed himself upright. It was a mistake. The room spun and Bishop's vision blurred once again. He collapsed back into the soft pillow.

"Woah there, cowboy."

A middle-aged nurse rushed towards him, placing his hand on Bishop's shoulder. "You've been in a car accident, mate. Best take it easy for a bit, yeah?"

With a nod, Bishop continued to lift himself from the hospital bed, ignoring the advice.

The nurse placed a surprisingly firm hand on his shoulder. "Heard you were a tough one. Listen, you're not going anywhere, mate."

Bishop pushed against the hand, attempting to shrug it off, but the nurse was having none of it. He pushed the spy back.

"I'll take a blood test, and I can be really bad at finding a vein."

Opening his mouth, Bishop released a hoarse wheeze. "That's not much of a threat."

The nurse raised an eyebrow. "Then I'll do the same with a catheter."

The two men stared at each other for the longest time.

Bishop frowned. "Maybe I'll stay here for a bit longer."

"Excellent choice, sir."

Letting loose an arid cough, Bishop flopped back into the bed. His mouth was drier than a long Saharan summer.

The nurse checked his chart. "Water's fine, hang on."

He filled a plastic cup from a water jug. Bishop downed it in one gulp and held it up for a refill.

"You'll wet the bed."

Bishop turned to see Paul enter. He wore his usual immaculate suit, but an unusual expression of concern. The nurse gave him a nod and left quietly.

"Where am I?" Bishop croaked.

"Barts. St Bartholomew's. Thought you'd like to be somewhere near home."

Bishop finished another cup of water. "The ambassador's dead." It was a statement, not a question.

Paul nodded. "They took out five police officers along the way. The Home Secretary is screaming blue murder. I can't blame her. This is tantamount to—"

"An act of war?"

"Precisely." Paul pulled up a chair. "What do you recall?"

Bishop gave a rundown of events, providing Paul with all the details he could remember.

"The one thing I don't get is why was I spared?"

"What makes you so special?" Paul gave a slight smirk. "I hate to tell you, my old chum, but I don't think you are."

"I have a contact list in my phone that'll tell you otherwise."

Paul rolled his eyes, no stranger to Bishop's justifiable boasting. "No, I mean whoever the sniper was, he was scared off by the locals. They heard the car crash and came running. If you hadn't made it to the road we wouldn't be having this quaint little chat. My guess is there were too many locals to pick off, so the shooter scarpered."

"The intruders' bodies at the mansion. Any IDs yet?"

"That's the trouble. There aren't any." The surprise must have been evident on Bishop's face. Paul went on. "No assailants were found in the mansion or in the grounds. The downed police, the ambassador and your sorry arse were all that was left. Well, there were several pools of blood. I suspected they were your handiwork."

"No evidence, no leads?"

"None. Except now we have your statement. MI5 and the Met will want you to repeat all that, of course. They'll most likely give you a medal, I suspect."

"Sod the fucking medal, give me the son of a bitch who did this. All I need is a soundproof room, a few hours, a filleting knife and some pliers." Bishop recognised the anger burning inside him. The dead police and the ambassador's lifeless stare swirled before his eyes. "Do we have anything on an arms dealer called Kali?" He explained what Demir had told him.

"We'll look into it." Paul blew out a lungful of air. "I hope it's not a new player. We thought we were doing so well on that front."

Bishop tilted his head inquisitively.

Paul went on. "In the last year or so we believed the illegal arms trade had decreased. A few high-profile dealers have either publicly retired or disappeared. Can't say we'll miss them terribly. Interpol have been taking credit for the downturn."

"Or maybe someone has taken over, and they're better at concealing their tracks."

"That's an unpleasant thought."

To distract himself, Bishop stretched and examined his arms.

As if reading his mind, Paul said, "Nothing broken. Some internal haemorrhaging, but nothing too vital. Some rest, some medication, and you'll be on your feet in a few days."

"You get me out of here today, Paul."

"I'm not sure that's …"

"Today."

It was generally ill-advised to raise one's voice with a

superior, but at that moment Bishop didn't give two shits about decorum.

"I'll see what I can do." Paul frowned at the request, but Bishop sensed there was more to his reaction. Perhaps a sense of pride that one of his own was so dedicated to the Service. If Paul felt that, it was fine, but he was wrong. It wasn't the job that fired Bishop. It was the thought of revenge.

"This anger… you seem so driven by all this." Paul seemed embarrassed, a rare occurrence. "Is it magnified, perhaps, because of Tessa?"

Bishop was taken aback. "How is this even remotely connected to her?" He realised too late the antagonism in his words.

"It's been two years—exactly two years. I remember, because exactly one year ago we were sozzled under a pool table in the Kings Arms. I thought perhaps the anniversary of her…"

"Dumping me and throwing my heart in a blender?"

"Yes, that." Paul was never comfortable talking about emotions. "I thought it might be playing on you."

Bishop hadn't realised it was the anniversary. In this instance his boss was way off. Had it only been two years? He'd spiralled into one-night stands without consequence or emotional entanglement. He closed himself off to any hint of intimacy. Over time he had built a solid ice wall around his heart to keep it from ever being hurt again. It had worked, but at a cost. The loneliness was the worst. Especially when he had a naked woman in the bed beside him and knew he'd never see her again. Tessa had hurt him like no one ever had, but she wasn't the one who had stoked this particular fire.

He needed to change the subject. After a deep sigh, Bishop shook his head. "Who the hell has the power to kill an ambassador under the protection of the Metropolitan Police?"

Paul's face was gravely serious. "That's what you're going to find out."

Listening to the sound of morning traffic outside his window, Bishop sighed. "What happens next?"

"We get you to Marrakech."

CHAPTER THREE

She was a woman men would have gone to war over in times past.

Bishop did his best not to stare.

Marrakech Menara Airport was architecturally striking. It made a grand first impression with its abundance of natural light, tastefully mixing modern and Moroccan styles. As Bishop sat in the airport bar, he ignored the remarkable space. Instead, he watched the woman walking down the causeway carrying a brown wide-brimmed hat and pulling her luggage. She stopped to talk with a porter, her long blonde hair swishing with even the slightest head movement.

Airport bars were the same the world over. Why had the Irish pub become the be all and end all of international travel? Why anyone would fly to Africa only to decide they absolutely needed to down an over-priced Guinness was beyond Bishop. But there he sat, propped up at the bar, indifferently taking in the passing parade as passengers flitted from one destination to another. Until she walked by.

Outside was a dry heat, but it was nothing compared

to what the woman in the sundress projected. She had a casual confidence, but it wasn't fuelled by her beauty. There was far more going on underneath the flawless skin. That was why Bishop was smitten from afar. Attractiveness only entertained for so long. When a woman had depth and intelligence to match, he found it hard to resist.

But resist he did. He was on a mission. His attention turned to an international rugby match on the pub's big screen. Wallabies versus the Springboks. After a disastrous lineout, the Springboks turned the ball over for a try. The Aussies were goners. When he glanced across the concourse again, the woman was gone. Just as well. There was too much at stake for distractions. Though there was nothing wrong with the occasional daydream.

While Bishop took a sip of his ghastly beer, a chubby, sunburnt gent with a garish shirt and even louder body odour flopped down two barstools away. He hefted an oversized cabin suitcase onto the seat between them.

When Bishop eyed him struggling with the case, the large gent gave him a puckish grin. "Spent a bit too much at the bazaar, I'm afraid." He had a South African accent.

"Easy to do. Any haggling tips?" Bishop asked.

"Keep your wife at home." The man gave an uproarious laugh.

Not finding the chauvinist remark remotely amusing, Bishop returned to his people-watching. The South African ordered a Miller Light and practically inhaled it.

But he wasn't South African. The two had traded the required code phrases to confirm their identities. The man was there to pass over the case containing Bishop's weapon and surveillance pack.

In a hushed tone, the man said, "I'm surprised they chose such a blunt instrument for this assignment."

Bishop maintained his disinterested expression. He

was careful not to peek at the other man, staring ahead. He didn't know this agent, nor did he know where his regular station was. He understood it wasn't Marrakech, because there was no station chief in the entire country. Whoever this was, he had a hide to insult a fellow agent he'd just met. Worse, an agent he'd just armed.

The trouble was, he was right. Bishop was a blunt instrument. As he'd mused back in Paul's office, his missions were either seduction or bloody wet work. This mission was neither. Was Paul preparing him for something greater, or was the operation of so little consequence it didn't matter who they assigned?

"A blunt instrument is still an instrument." Bishop sipped his beer. "It will get the job done."

In the reflection of the glass fridge across the bar, Bishop saw the man sneer. "A hammer sees everything as a nail."

"True. But you can still hammer a nail after you bludgeon a man to death with it." Bishop risked his cover by giving the man a quick sideways glance before gazing forward again. "Or torture a man by breaking every bone in his hand until he splutters what you need to know. The hammer will get the job done."

The other agent grunted. "I fly out in an hour. You won't need anything else."

It was a statement, not an offer.

Bishop shrugged. "Charmed."

He plodded off, leaving Bishop with the tab for his drink. Bishop wasn't sad to see him go. It appeared he had a reputation. He wasn't entirely happy about that.

Finishing his beer, the MI6 agent left a pile of dirham on the counter and headed towards the exit, new bag in tow. The outside heat was a pleasant sultry surprise after the chilled confines of the airport. Dodging the ride spruikers offering transport into Marrakech, Bishop headed towards the taxi rank. As a spy, he'd learned long ago that any of the non-official drivers could be an enemy. The randomness of selecting the next taxi diminished the likelihood of running into any representative of the opposite side—in this case, Kali. At least, that was the theory.

The airport was only 10 kilometres from the centre of Marrakech, so it wouldn't be long before he could check into his hotel. The five taxi bays were empty, the long metal barriers designed to herd queues of waiting passengers seeming overly optimistic. Two uniformed airport staff waited to shepherd the crowd—Bishop—to the next available vehicle. He was the line. With no choice but to wait, Bishop rocked on his heels.

He'd probably have to get used to waiting. It was questionable that there was an enemy to confront at all. The only source of intelligence was the ambassador, and he was dead. It was completely possible that Demir had been deceived, or even that he had lied. If the mission turned out to be a complete waste, maybe Bishop could try and find the blonde to console him.

"Hi."

Bishop turned to see a brown wide-brimmed hat. Underneath was the stunning blonde, with the bluest eyes he'd ever seen.

"Speak of the devil."

Amusingly taken aback, the woman replied, "I'm sorry?" She had an upper crust English accent.

"Forgive me." Bishop composed himself. "I meant to say, good afternoon." He flashed the wide grin that had served him so well in the past.

The woman could have powered the entire continent with the intensity of the smile she gave him in return. It was spectacular. Up close she was even more striking than he would have thought possible.

"This is a little…" She was embarrassed, which Bishop suspected was a rarity. "I was wondering if you'd like to share a cab to Marrakech. You know, single woman, travelling alone and all…"

The use of the word cab meant she'd either spent time abroad or watched too many American TV shows.

"What makes you think I'm remotely trustworthy?" Bishop gave her a roguish grin.

"You dress far too well to be too much of a creep."

"Ah, but surely they're the ones your mother warned you about? A well-dressed wolf is still a wolf."

"My mother never warned me about a man who wears a Gieves & Hawkes suit."

Bishop nodded, impressed. "You seem well-versed in fashion, Miss…?"

"Astrid Spencer." She extended a hand. "You'd be most amazed at what I'm well versed in, Mister…?"

Bishop shook her hand. Her grip was delicate, but firm. "Langford. Tyler Langford." He gave his mission alias. "I have a feeling I would not be at all surprised by what you are well versed in, Ms Spencer. Not at all." He took a pleasant moment to gaze into her dazzling eyes.

"You want taxi?" one of the uniformed airport staff asked.

"I was actually waiting for tickets to the Cirque du Soleil," Bishop replied, "but a taxi would be lovely, thank you."

Astrid laughed. It wasn't a girly giggle, but a mature, full-throated laugh. She didn't cover her mouth by way of apology, as some women did. She owned it. She found it amusing, responded and found it nothing she should apologise for. Bishop was smitten.

The attendant waved his arms to flag a taxi.

Turning his attention to Astrid, Bishop tilted his head downwards. "I would love to share a taxi, but alas, I'm not going your way. I'm heading away from the city to Essaouira for some much-needed R and R. I must say I regret my life choices at this very moment, but there you are."

Astrid made no attempt to conceal her disappointment, but politely nodded. "Such a shame, Mr Langford. I dare say our trip would have been a most pleasant one…"

In a flurry of hand movements, the two unformed airport staff waved at an approaching taxi as if it would somehow drive on by if not hurriedly flagged down. It pulled to a stop before them and Bishop opened the door for Astrid.

She handed the airport staff a few dirham and cast Bishop an impish smile. "To thoughts of what may have been, Mr Langford."

As the taxi drove off she gave him a wink. Bishop turned to the two airport workers, who gawped at him as if he was the stupidest man alive. He very well may have been.

Another thing Bishop had learned as a spy was that when something seemed too good to be true, it probably was. Normally, Bishop preferred the role of the predator. In his past life, the non-spy one, he'd quite enjoyed being the prey too. But not now. The life of a spy meant he had to be wary of being approached. The lovely lady's invitation may have been innocent, but he could never be sure. It was the doubt that made him politely decline. In espionage, the unknown got you killed.

The drive into Marrakech was uneventful. Bishop's driver, Amare, was a good-humoured family man who knew all about the city. He was unaware, however, of any auction or villa owned by a Frenchman called Temple. They spoke of the upcoming World Cup for the remainder of the short trip.

Checking into the luxurious Mandarin Oriental under the name of Langford, Bishop was shown to his room. Once he'd tipped the porter for showing him where all the perfectly visible light switches were, he locked the door behind him.

When he opened the case he'd been slipped at the airport, he found an envelope on top of the foam-packed weapons and gear. Extracting a single piece of paper from it, Bishop saw that it held a series of squiggles and dots. He activated his mobile phone and opened the cloaked MI6 app. The meaningless scratching on the page morphed into words.

Welcome, Bishop. We have investigated further and can confirm there is a villa owned by one Lucas Temple. Immigration has him currently out of the country, but I wouldn't rely on that. He claims to be a geologist, but we can find no qualification to support this claim. Below are the exact coordinates. Due to lack of local agents, no surveillance has yet been conducted. We have no information on an auction, nor do Five Eyes. No unusual activity, no additional chatter on undesirable channels.

Your report expected daily at 17:00 local time. If extraction needed, best case scenario would be six to eight hours, so I suggest not getting involved in any sticky situations. You're basically on your own. Good luck, try not to get shot.

PC

Paul's mix of stern authority and flippancy amused Bishop. So there was an actual Temple. Perhaps this mission wasn't a wash after all. Shame, he'd been looking forward to chasing down the blonde, who could have been anywhere in the sprawling city. Alas, King and Country beckoned.

Bishop burned the paper in the kitchen sink, then went to the bathroom to wash off the slick coating that always came from travelling. He shaved and dressed in more appropriate warm weather attire. The linen suit and patterned shirt were a pleasing mix of formal and relaxed, suiting his cover of a well-to-do tourist. Suitably refreshed, he made his way to the bank of elevators.

After pressing the down button, Bishop went through the next few hours in his mind. Conduct surveillance on Temple's villa, reconnoitre the surrounding area, gather intelligence where possible. Sensing someone approaching, he did his best to appear a casual holidaymaker while preparing for any eventuality.

"You must have an absolutely terrible sense of direction." The voice was silky smooth.

Bishop turned to see a tall, slim figure standing beside him, sunhat in hand, a light muslin shawl over her tanned, flawless skin. Astrid had a towel under her arm, dressed for the pool.

He hadn't prepared for this particular eventuality.

There was a *ping*, the doors opened and the pair entered the empty elevator.

"Essaouira is that way." She pointed to the right and raised a playful eyebrow. "About 200 kilometres." Her face was practically saying, *talk your way out of this one, chum.*

"My plans changed," Bishop said, good-humoured.

"You don't say?" Astrid attempted to scowl, but soon broke into a smirk. "I'm not used to being brushed off, Mr Langford." She took a moment, as if rolling the idea around in her head. "I must say, it's an interesting experience."

"Let me make it up to you." Bishop spoke without thinking it through, which was a rarity. What was it about this woman? "I have some errands to take care of this afternoon. Perhaps I could buy you a cocktail in the lounge, say six o'clock?"

She pursed her lips. "Fine. But if you stand me up again I'll hunt you down and make you pay. I paid for a whole six months' worth of karate lessons, so you'd better watch out."

"How many classes did you attend?"

"Three, so you'd better turn up or else." She thrust a fist in his face. It was as terrifying as a bunny nibbling on a carrot.

Bishop held up two palms. "Whatever you do, don't hurt me. I'll be there. Scout's honour."

"Ever been in the Scouts?"

"Not even three times."

The elevator doors opened on level two, where a sign advised that the pool was to the left. Astrid stepped out of the elevator and turned to Bishop. As the doors slid closed, she waggled her fist and screwed her face up adorably.

Bishop chuckled and shook his head. She certainly had a way about her, but he was still cautious. He had to be. She was just a little too perfect. Meeting her again could be a coincidence. Then again, he could have been made.

Yet he had invited her for a drink. If Astrid was an enemy agent, he didn't want to arouse suspicion. If she wasn't, then a completely different set of arousal could be in order.

〜

The word "villa" could account for many types of dwelling, from a humble shack to a near-mansion. Lucas Temple's erred on the latter side, and then some. Like the others in the neighbourhood, it was surrounded by a 10-foot-high fence. The exclusive suburb of Palmeraie offered a stunning view of the high Atlas Mountains to the south. But Bishop wasn't interested in the views. His interests were more inward looking.

Taking his time to walk around the perimeter fence several times, Bishop didn't notice anything unusual. There were no security cameras, no external motion detectors, floodlights or security system of any description to suggest that this was a house of great strategic importance. It seemed just like many of the others in the luxurious estate.

Finding a local convenience store, Bishop bought a six pack of Pepsi, some brown paper, sticky tape and a pen. Outside the store, he wrapped the six pack in the brown paper and wrote Temple's address on it.

He approached the front gate and pressed the intercom button. No reply. He tried three more times, but each request received the same stony response. So much for Plan A.

The gate was secured by a stock standard Yale lock. It took Bishop all of three seconds to crack it open using his bump key. The gate swung silently forward on its hinges. Bishop waited. No guard dogs.

Aware he couldn't stay at the gate for too long without arousing suspicion, he stepped into the grounds. If discovered, he would argue that the gate had opened all by itself, so he had assumed they wanted him to come to the front door. There was no need for subterfuge. It seemed the villa and its grounds were devoid of life. He closed the gate.

A square swimming pool graced the front of the sand-coloured single storey mansion. Palm trees surrounded it, creating the feeling of an oasis. The villa itself was ornately decorated in the Moroccan style, but with a modern twist.

Bishop knocked on the huge ornate front doors, for good measure. Again, there was no answer. With the use of the bump key, he was in. Inside, the mansion was much the same as outside. Spacious, opulent and dripping with excess. Not Bishop's style, but he wasn't here to buy the place.

He took his time investigating, but turned up little of interest, unless he counted the well-stocked wine cellar. The Château d'Yquem was a particular highlight. Temple knew his wines, Bishop had to give him that. For all intents and purposes, Temple's villa was simply a nice, luxurious residence.

Except it wasn't.

On the verge of giving up, Bishop noticed something odd. The kitchen pantry seemed smaller than it should be. The wall it backed onto in the hall seemed too far away, given the size of the pantry. It took some time, but Bishop found the lever, and the blank wall silently slid away to reveal a thin set of steps.

Extracting his pistol, Bishop descended the dark stairs. Below ground level was a sparse, dimly lit room. The bare brick walls and earthen floor were not as stylishly decorated as the rooms above. This room seemed to serve another purpose. A far more sinister one.

At the centre of the room sat a wooden table. In each corner of the table, solid metal shackles dangled from chains. Carved gullies around the edge reminded Bishop of an autopsy table. The channels led to a hole in the corner of the table, which sat above a metal receptacle was stained various shades of red. On a small stand, surgical-sharp implements sat on a red velvet cloth. The dark crimson stains on the floor told the spy that the room had been used many times.

It seemed Mr Temple was no simple geologist. This man was a sadist. A torturer. How did this relate to Demir and the dead body on Westminster Bridge? Bishop may have been a blunt instrument, but he was a blunt instrument determined to find out what the hell was going on.

CHAPTER FOUR

After making his way back to the hotel, Bishop filed a quick report. He advised that he'd return to the villa tomorrow and install surveillance devices, particularly in the customised subterranean not-at-all-games room. After that he cleaned up and changed. It wouldn't do to turn up for his drink with Astrid dressed all in black and smelling like he'd been skulking around in basements. There was an etiquette to such things.

Heading down to the ground floor bar, he checked his watch. He was late, but only by fifteen minutes or so. As Bishop strode across the opulent lobby, he spotted Astrid instantly. She wasn't a woman you could miss, clad in a flattering light blue sundress that was tasteful but managed to compliment all the right curves.

She wasn't alone.

Beside her sat a man. Well, less a man, more a leer in human form—scruffy, dishevelled, with a three-day growth. He was rough, with a slightly ugly crooked nose, but in a way that could appeal to women. Like the ten minutes in the nineties when Gérard Depardieu had been considered handsome.

When Bishop approached, Astrid's mouth slanted in a half smirk. "You're late."

"No I'm not." Bishop tilted his watch at her. "I'm exactly on time, give or take."

"Give or take?" She failed to hide her amusement.

Bishop gave a shrug. "I'm more of a giver."

"Really, because from here it seems like you're taking the piss."

The scruffy man, who had been following the conversation, pointed a finger between the two of them. "Ah. Banter."

His accent was as thick as day-old borscht. He frowned as he listened, as if following intently, trying to translate.

"And whom might this be?" Bishop asked as he sat. He waved to a nearby waiter.

"My name is Mikhail."

Astrid extended her hand to the scruffy man beside her and introduced herself.

"Tyler." Bishop nodded to the other man, pleased the two hadn't gotten as far as social niceties. "You two just met?"

"Yes, Mikhail just sat down." She rose a challenging eyebrow. "He arrived just in time, unlike others I could mention."

Bishop ignored the bait and regarded the big man. "Mikhail? Russian?"

"Da."

When the waiter arrived, Bishop ordered a whiskey sour. The other two were nursing their drinks; a tropical sweet thing in a tall glass for Astrid, and what, comically, appeared to be a Black Russian for him. If this was the sixties, Bishop's spy senses would have been tingling. Then again, even the KGB wouldn't be stupid enough to throw a heavily accented Russian on an undercover mission.

When his drink arrived, Bishop knew immediately it was a sub-par beverage. A good whiskey sour took time and care. This one had arrived so quickly he doubted it would bear any resemblance to its namesake. He took a sip. It didn't. Not wanting to make a scene, he addressed his drinking compatriots.

"Isn't this cosy?" His smile was so strained you could have drained pasta through it.

"You have heard saying three's company?" Mikhail asked with scorn.

Astrid giggled. "I think you mean three's a crowd?"

With a frown, Mikhail replied, "Yes, that too. Very crowded here." His eyes narrowed in on Bishop.

Bishop brushed non-existent lint from his shirt. "Have you heard the saying if you can't handle the heat get out of the kitchen?"

Mikhail positively scowled. "Have you heard saying, После драки кулаками не машут?" When silence was the only response, he added, "Is Russian saying, may not translate well. Means do not swing fists when the fight is over."

"Down, boys." Astrid raised an eyebrow at them. "We're all friends here. I'll decide who I spend time with. Now," she slapped her hands together, "let's get to know each other."

For the next few minutes, the "friends" exchanged the requisite boring crib notes on their lives. Bishop stuck to his mission persona of a holidaying account executive of a mid-level London advertising firm. Mikhail was on his way to a construction trade conference in Johannesburg and had convinced his employer he deserved a few extra days in Marrakech because he hadn't taken leave in five years. Astrid was celebrating the anniversary of her divorce by taking a holiday to a destination her ex never would have gone to.

If he were a cynical man, and he was, Bishop would have called all their stories gossamer thin to the point of incredulity. Then again, perhaps this was how regular people talked. It had been many years since he'd been able to socialise with regular people without double-thinking their every motive.

Astrid lit up the room with every word, every gesture. The woman was dazzling. Skilled as a courtesan, she could have men hanging off her every word. She was too engaging, too beautiful, too lovely.

That was one reason Bishop would finish his drink, graciously bow out and head back to his room alone. Astrid was too good to be true. There were few men who could evade her charms, thereby making her the perfect fit for espionage. Her flawlessness made Bishop wary. There had been missions where he hadn't paid heed to uneasiness and it had cost him and others dearly.

The other reason was, even if she was who she said she was, he was on a mission and that must take priority. That, and he had no desire to go head to head with Mikhail, fighting for Astrid's affections like two dogs tussling over the last bone in the yard. He had his pride, after all, even though he knew it was a fight he would win.

Finishing the last of his drink, Bishop placed the glass on the table. "Well, this has been lovely. I'm afraid I have an early start in the morning, so I'll need to wish you both good night."

"You're leaving?" Astrid's pained expression almost made him waver, but he held strong.

"Okay, bye bye." Mikhail seemed rather keen for him to leave.

Bishop addressed Astrid. "I am most sorry, but alas, I

have to be off to Essaouira as I can't put it off any longer. My transfer leaves at an ungodly hour."

"Too bad." Mikhail scanned the bar for a waiter. "Bye bye."

"And here I thought I had two gents tussling for my attention." Astrid pouted. "What does a girl have to do to have fun around here, put herself up for auction to the highest bidder?"

Mikhail's head snapped around, as did Bishop's. The word "auction" was fraught.

"That's an unusual choice of words, I must say."

"I feel like I was going to be auctioned off." Astrid shrugged at Bishop. "But if one disappears, no auction, I guess."

There was a knowingness to her smile, a glint in her eye. Perhaps Bishop's wariness was right after all. The woman seemed too perfect for a reason.

Bishop waved to the waiter, ordering another round. "Perhaps I could stay for one more."

It was interesting how similar Mikhail's reaction had been to his. Were they both here for the auction? Were all three here for the same reason? Or had one or more obtained an invitation, like Demir?

Either way, Bishop wasn't going anywhere. He took off his jacket.

"I'm glad you stayed. The more the merrier, given my stalker."

Bishop was alarmed. "Your what?"

"I think that's what he is." She smiled an ethereally thin smile. "I've seen this bloke around, at the pool, when I was at the bazaar, about four times, maybe five. Doesn't come close, doesn't say or do anything, he's just there. Super weird."

"Build?" Bishop's eyes darted around the hotel bar, searching for suspicious characters.

51

"Slim. Weedy. Not like you two gents." She attempted to be bright and cheerful, but failed miserably. "Haven't seen his face properly, he wears this grey hood. I'm not crazy to think it's not normal, am I? That's all pretty creepy, right?"

"Da, creepy," Mikhail agreed indifferently, and poked the ice in his drink.

Bishop had seen a grey-hooded figure of his own rather recently, although his had been holding a sniper rifle. It was concerning.

When the drinks arrived, Bishop began assessing the two with clearer eyes. Mikhail's interest in Astrid seemed to have doubled since she uttered the word "auction". The news of a hooded figure in Marrakech was troubling. It also complicated matters.

He needed to talk to Astrid alone. That meant Bishop would need to follow up on his earlier theoretical confidence and win Astrid's affections before the big Russian did. It seemed the two dogs would go head to head after all.

The waiter took away the tray of empty shot glasses with concern in his eyes. It wasn't concern for their wellbeing, it was because the three rowdy guests had been steadily scaring off patrons for the last three hours.

Bishop picked up another shot glass and waved an accusatory finger at Astrid. "That is a scandalous, unmitigated thing to say! If you were a man I'd take you outside and thrash you."

"If I were a man," her words slurred, "the topic wouldn't have come up."

Bishop waved the glass about ponderously. "Good

point." He downed the shot and slammed the glass on the table.

Mikhail hiccupped and contemplated the shot glass as if it contained the very meaning of existence. Mikhail and Astrid were far more inebriated than Bishop. He was feigning most of his drunkenness. The other two were either as good at concealing their sobriety as Bishop, or they really were three sheets to the wind.

Astrid swayed her glass. "All I'm shaying—"

"Did you just say shaying?"

"— is in my experience it's overrated." Even with the volume of drink she'd consumed, there was a coyness to her comment, embarrassment. Astrid's face flushed, spreading all the way down to her cleavage. "In my experience. Is what I meant."

Bishop was incredulous. "Cunnilingus is overrated? My dear lady, I do hope you're not serious."

For the first time, Astrid was unable to meet his eyes. She placed her hands demurely in her lap. "In my experience, yes." It didn't seem to be an act, she actually seemed sincere. Bishop tried not to gape.

Mikhail belched. It was unclear if it was gas or a precursor to being sick. All three had been downing drinks at an alarming rate. Despite his best intentions to steer the conversation to any kind of auction talk, the others, tactfully or otherwise, had navigated away. Bishop decided the only way to determine what Astrid knew was to take her away from Mikhail. It was time to utilise one of his main skills, and it wasn't being a blunt instrument.

"I think," Mikhail raised a stately finger.

He belched again and the finger withered. The big man slunk into his seat. He was down, and it was time for Bishop to go in for the kill.

"Look, I know what this is going to sound like,

believe me, but my dear woman if you genuinely believe that, you've been dating the wrong people your entire adult life. This ex-husband of yours was a fool, and an incompetent one at that."

Astrid shifted in her chair. When he'd first sat down, she had held court, dominated the table and conversation. Now there was a subtle change in her demeanour. He'd managed to pique her interest. Shifting her shapely behind in the chair, she relaxed her shoulders, leaned slightly closer and stroked her hair. Tiny moves, individually indicating nothing. But combined, they sent signal flares into the chilly Moroccan night air.

For a moment, Bishop remained silent, allowing her to plunge into her thoughts for a while. The faraway expression in her eyes told him she was enjoying the exercise.

When her gaze returned to his, he decided to push his luck. Ignoring Mikhail, he subtly moved his fingers to gently caress the bare flesh of her leg, finding it as smooth and warm as it appeared. She didn't recoil, she didn't scream, she didn't slap his hand away. Mikhail had his eyes closed and swayed from side to side.

Astrid stared at him for the longest time and bit her lip.

Silence would no longer cut it. If this encounter was to progress, he needed to utilise the advantage.

"Let me tell you something," he murmured, just loud enough for her to hear.

He bent forward, and she mirrored his move. He didn't look away from her bright blue eyes. Mere inches from each other, Bishop tilted his head ever so slightly, his one-day stubble gently brushing her cheek, lips tantalisingly close to her delicate skin. Her breath hitched and her soft cheek nuzzled his.

In a husky voice he whispered, "The tongue is a sometimes-neglected muscle, often disregarded at the expense of its lumbering, more stupid, harder brother." It was a statement she was sure to associate with the big Russian beside them. "A powerful implement, but capable of such delicate feather-light caresses, it is quite remarkable. And versatile. Did I mention versatile? Capable of lapping, swirling and penetrating, it's more than qualified to taste all the succulent delights afforded to it. It is multitalented, and having no immediate end goal, the tongue can linger for as long as required and relentlessly pursue its goal again and again and again, until it's begged to stop." Straightening his back, Bishop resumed his normal speaking voice. "Like I said, versatile."

What could only be described as a slow, throaty purr emanated from Astrid. Gone was the plastic shell of an unattainable goddess. It had been replaced by a woman consumed by one thing.

Pure lust.

She stood and picked up her handbag. Her legs wobbled slightly. Bishop was unsure if it was the drink or his words that had made her unsteady. He did his best to keep his expression neutral, to avoid giving away the pleasure of victory. Bishop prepared himself for the next few hours with Astrid. Sometimes his job did offer the most tantalising perks.

"Mikhail." Astrid shook the big Russian's shoulder to wake him. "Tyler and I are heading up to my room." She turned to Bishop with a wicked grin. "You're coming too."

The floor seemed to drop from beneath Bishop's feet. "What? Him too? I thought…"

"You thought after your nice little speech you were going to have me all to yourself?" She tutted and gave a playful shake of her head. "You forget, Mr Langford, as I mentioned earlier, I choose whoever I wish to spend my time with. Right now, I want you both. It's very simple, really. That is, unless you don't want to know my secrets?"

My god, this woman is good. Bishop shook his head. "Do you always get what you want?"

"Yes. Always." She lifted a challenging eyebrow. "Don't tell me you don't think you'll measure up?"

Bishop couldn't stifle the chuckle that escaped his lips. "I think you'll find, my good lady, I don't have any fears in that department."

"Cocky."

"Exactly."

～

The trip up to Astrid's floor was conducted in silence, each party lost in their own thoughts. Perhaps Mikhail was right? Three could be company.

Bishop eyed the Russian. The MI6 agent had been in a respectable number of threesomes, but always with two women, sometimes more. But never a devil's threesome. The thought didn't disgust or intimidate him; it was the thought of Mikhail's involvement that irked him.

Bishop had to accept Astrid's invitation. Refusing to include the Russian may have caused Astrid to change her mind, or worse, to leave with Mikhail instead. The fact that she was in Marrakech and had used the word auction so freely piqued his interest. There was far more going on than she let on. It was unfortunate that he wouldn't have her to himself, but being a spy meant being adaptive. That's what he intended to do.

He also intended to do something else; avoid eye contact with Mikhail.

The three entered the dimly lit room quietly. A single Moroccan lamp in the corner of the large suite gave the room an otherworldly feel. As expected, it wasn't long before Astrid took charge and had both men in hand. There was an audible gasp when Bishop presented his credentials, and not just from Astrid.

For the next two hours the three writhed on the bed in one sweaty, lustful mass. They pushed one another beyond their known boundaries, then collapsed, sated and exhausted.

Mikhail tapped out the earliest, and lay at the far end of the king-sized bed, snoring loudly. Astrid rested her head on Bishop's chest, finally able to catch her breath.

"I take back what I said before. Not," she ran her fingers through his chest hair, "overrated."

"The gentleman in me prevents me from saying I told you so."

The dimples came out in her face when she smiled. "Just as well." She kissed his chest.

They lay there for some time. Bishop walked through the night's actions in his mind. It was a pleasant stroll. It wasn't the only thing on his mind.

"You seemed to handle the situation well." She quietly chuckled. "The additional presence, I mean. I'm glad I wasn't auctioned off. I think it's far better to share, don't you?"

"There's that word again." He kept his voice low, so as not to wake their companion.

"Share?"

"No. Auction. It's like you're teasing me with it."

"You're rather adept at teasing yourself, Mr Langford." Her finger traced a path on his chest. "You had me on a string there, I must say. You… you know how to hold a woman's attention. That's quite a talent."

"Excellent evasion there." Bishop tried to keep his tone playful. "But you avoided my point about an auction. Seems to be on your mind. I'm wondering why?"

Astrid pulled at his chest hair, eliciting a roguish yelp. "A woman pays a man a compliment, possibly the best compliment she could, and you change the subject?"

"I changed nothing," Bishop protested. "Seems you're the one avoiding the question."

Astrid propped herself up on one elbow, her left breast resting on his chest. She gazed into his eyes. "Careful, Mr Langford. A regular woman could become concerned she was being interrogated."

"Lucky you're an extraordinary woman then, isn't it?" He lifted his hand to caress her cheek.

"I... it's dangerous for me to talk about..." She turned away, uncomfortable. It was a rare sign of vulnerability in a woman usually so confident. "I shouldn't keep saying... I wondered if you were here for... it's just scary to be part of... things." Her eyes contained genuine fear.

"Perhaps I can help? If you're in danger..."

"Please... I shouldn't have said anything. Forget it. Please forget it. Forget me."

Bishop did his best to stifle his laugh. "I assure you, unless I'm hit in the head with a rather large mallet, it is not humanly possible to forget you."

Her fingers brushed his lips. "You're sweet. But please, drop it for now. For me."

"I can help."

"What could a humble advertising executive do?"

"My dear lady, I think we both know I'm not... humble." That elicited a smile. Bishop ran his thumb across her chin. "I think we also both know I'm more than an executive. If you're in over your head, I want you to know I can help."

She nodded, her brow furrowed. Astrid rested her

head on his chest. "Drop it, please. For your sake." She sighed. "We should sleep."

Not wanting to push it and risk scaring her off, Bishop decided to drop it, for now. He would question her again as soon as he was able. He closed his eyes. That was when Bishop realised Mikhail had stopped snoring.

In the early morning light, Bishop rolled over and sighed. The gentle rise and fall of Astrid's chest and her serene face as she slept filled him with a yearning he had scarcely known. Not for a long time. Not since Tessa. Astrid was an exception, and an exceptional one at that. He studied her face. Even in its imperfections he found perfection. *This woman.*

The tranquil scene was ripped apart by the shrill sound of the hotel telephone. Astrid sat up with a start. Bishop's exquisite view was abruptly replaced by Mikhail's ugly face staring right back at him. Both men rolled over to face the other way.

Astrid muttered, "Yes, thank you," and hung up. She turned to Bishop. "Wake-up call."

Startled that she'd slept so long, she plunged into the bathroom for an ultra-fast freshen up. She emerged minutes later, only slightly less dishevelled. Paying little heed to her outfit selection, she flung on clothes, not turning away as she dressed. After the night before, there was no need for modesty.

"Where are you headed?" Bishop did his best to sound casual.

"I... that thing we... didn't really discuss?" She pulled her hair into a ponytail. "There's something I need to... I won't be back for a couple of hours."

Before Bishop could say more, in quick succession she

kissed Mikhail and then him. She took a moment to assess her conquests. "I feel I need to commemorate this somehow." Her face creased into a wicked smile.

"Do we get parting gifts?" Bishop asked.

Astrid snapped her fingers in agreement and glanced about the hotel room. She handed Mikhail the "Do Not Disturb" door hanger they had miraculously failed to utilise the night before. Approaching Bishop's side of the bed, her eyes sparkled as she handed him her "gift".

"A pen?"

It was emblazoned with the words "Mandarin Oriental" on the side.

She shrugged. "It's mightier than a sword."

"So they say."

She leaned down and kissed his cheek, taking a moment to linger beside him. Before she broke the embrace, he slid his cover's business card in her palm. In a whisper, Bishop said, "Call me as soon as you're able. We need to talk."

Astrid looked him directly in the eye and gave a firm nod. She understood. There was gratitude in her eyes, and it wasn't due to the previous night's activities. Perhaps she saw Bishop as a way out of whatever was scaring her. That was good. He was close to finding what it was all about, and if he could help Astrid along the way, that would make it all the sweeter.

The hotel door closed, and Bishop and Mikhail took their cue. They dressed and left without a word to one another.

Back in the comfort of his own hotel room, Bishop took the longest shower he could remember. Cleaned and changed, he headed back to Temple's villa. There were unanswered questions there, too.

The morning had a dry warmth that seemed deceptively fresh. Stray dogs trotted about the dusty streets as if they wanted to get all their affairs in order before the afternoon heat. Smart dogs.

Bishop took twenty minutes to scope the property, detecting no sign of life within. As he did so, his mind wandered. His thoughts returned to the events of the previous evening, and in particular, his conversation with Astrid. He couldn't be sure it was The Auction that she was talking about, but it seemed likely. And she seemed genuinely fearful about whatever her involvement was. How was she embroiled in international arms trading? And why had she attracted the attention of a grey-hooded stalker who just happened to match the description of the sniper who had taken out Demir? Bishop hoped to hear from her soon to find out.

Once again, Bishop created the pretence of a package delivery and picked the lock to enter. Again, no one stopped him wandering the grounds of the compound. No one answered the door, nor did anyone stop him from picking the lock and slipping inside.

This time he had extra baggage with him. Bishop had his surveillance pack, and he intended to use it.

Starting with the kitchen, Bishop planted the latest MI6 monitoring devices. Miniature ones for dark corners that could be hidden in air vents and smoke detectors; larger higher-definition devices in lampshades and bookshelves. He tested them as he went. They all worked perfectly.

He moved on to the bedrooms and bathrooms, then finally found his way into the subterranean torture chamber. Like the rest of the house, everything was as he'd left it; there was no suggestion that anyone had been there since the day before. He planted four devices in total in the room downstairs, more than he had in any other room. Bishop wanted to be sure that whatever occurred in this room was recorded.

Making his way upstairs, Bishop performed one last test of the equipment. Everything passed. *The boffins at MI6 really don't receive enough credit.* Closing his case, he performed one final reconnoitre to ensure he had left no evidence behind.

While in the kitchen, Bishop heard a scraping sound. Extracting his pistol, he was on high alert. Had Temple returned? Was it a housekeeper? Security?

He steadied his breathing and strained to hear more. He didn't have to wait long. Though muffled, there was a patter above his head. That was no bird. Someone was on the roof, fiddling with the skylight.

Mind racing as to where he could hide, Bishop decided that being cornered in the dungeon would be less than ideal. Then he mused. Owners rarely enter their property via their own skylight. If someone was on the roof, they were either performing maintenance up there or…

A shadow fell across the skylight. There was the hum of an electric drill, then it was lifted open. A heavy bag was dropped to the kitchen floor, right in front of Bishop. It landed with *clang*, as though it contained tools. Bishop backed into the butler's pantry, holding his weapon skyward, and waited.

A rope dropped from the ceiling and landed on the tiled floor. Definitely not the owner.

After several light grunts, someone descended. The strong arms made simple work of the climb, as if used to such physical exertion. When the person's feet reached the floor, there was an audible sigh.

Bishop didn't wait. He stepped forward and placed his gun to the intruder's head.

Pressing the barrel into the man's temple, Bishop moved close to his ear, voice like granite. "Nice of you to drop in, Mikhail."

CHAPTER FIVE

Bishop had the drop, but the big man had lightning-fast reactions. Brutally so. Not losing a moment to shock, the Russian dipped his head and wove his bulky fist on the inside of Bishop's gun arm, deflecting the weapon away. Ready for the move, Bishop stepped back and countered easily, using his feet to neutralise Mikhail's movement. Fighting was all about footwork. Gene Kelly would have been a hell of a brawler.

The big Russian drew his right fist back for a punch. Bishop tilted his upper body in anticipation, but Mikhail was messing with him. Two swift left jabs to Bishop's jaw meant his opposition had purposely telegraphed the first punch to get the next two in.

Damn. The guy had game. *Fine. No more fucking around.*

Wary of underestimating his opponent, Bishop circled the intruder around the kitchen, waiting for his next move. He seemed unperturbed by the gun, assuming that if Bishop hadn't fired yet, he was unlikely to. He was right. The man could have vital information. It was likely he was working against Temple. If so, he knew more than Bishop. That meant Bishop couldn't kill him.

It didn't mean he couldn't shoot him a little bit.

Mikhail bounded towards him, left arm up defensively, his footwork better this time. A big meaty fist flew towards Bishop as if propelled by rockets. Barely moving his head away in time, Bishop was about to use the big man's momentum against him. But the Russian had already shifted his body mass, readying himself for the next series of punches. He was learning.

Getting in a flurry of upper body blows, Bishop pushed the other man away, then held his hands up, palms wide. "Look, can I—"

The jab to the nose jerked Bishop's head backwards and he staggered.

"Listen, you crazy Ruskie, all I want to do is—"

This time a blow to the stomach doubled him over. Bishop managed to slide out of the way of the next punch but wheezed hard at the effort. Why didn't he want to talk? More to the point, why did Bishop want to? Was he doing this because it was what the opposite of a blunt instrument would do? Or was it what was best for the mission? Maybe it was both.

"We don't need to fight." Bishop ducked a lazy haymaker.

Mikhail huffed. "Why do you want to chat like an old woman?" His big fist missed Bishop's face but connected with his shoulder, sending him back two strides.

"It's new for me, I'm trying it out."

Unaffected by Bishop's words, Mikhail moved in for his next go, a series of upper body punches. While none of them were decisive blows, they weren't exactly love taps either. But they brought him in close.

Using his footwork to slide into position, Bishop kicked the inside of the big man's knee. The placement was less about force, more about precise pressure points. With a grunt, Mikhail buckled. Bishop smashed the grip of his pistol into Mikhail's forehead, sending the Russian reeling backwards until he landed heavily against the kitchen cabinet.

"Stay down, you stupid bastard. I'm trying to talk to you."

Mikhail nodded, but launched himself at Bishop once again. Not wanting to shoot him, the MI6 agent picked up the closest object. A large metal spatula. As his opponent attacked, Bishop weaved his body away and slapped the spatula clean across his face.

Mikhail stopped, and took a moment to register what had happened. "Did you just hit me with a kitchen implement?"

Once the shock had dripped from his face, he raised his meaty fists again. In response, Bishop smacked each hand with the spatula, like a mother who'd caught a kid trying to sneak cookies. He followed this up a slap on each cheek for good measure.

The Russian recoiled, his arms flailing wildly. "Stop hitting me with that thing!"

Taking full note of the request, Bishop stepped forward and flicked the spatula fast against Mikhail's forehead. It made a pleasing *boing* sound. The Russian staggered backwards.

Exasperated, Bishop asked, "Are we going to talk or do I have to get out a whisk?"

Bishop could see the cogs turning in the Russian's brain. He seemed extremely keen to attack again. The MI6 agent put down the spatula and aimed his gun. Mikhail sneered, but didn't attack. Seconds ticked by. The two men faced off.

Bishop considered the rope dangling from the

skylight. "I'm going out on a limb here, but I'm guessing you're not a construction worker?"

With his thumb, Mikhail wiped blood away from the corner of his mouth. "What are you doing here, Englishman?"

"Where I come from, it's the one holding the gun who asks the questions."

The Russian snorted. "And where is it you are from, little man?"

"I think we've established I don't quite deserve that label, wouldn't you say?"

Every muscle in the Russian tensed as he stared at Bishop. Good. If this was to turn into an interrogation, Bishop needed him angry. Angry men made far more mistakes than calm ones.

Taking a moment to admire Bishop's weapon, Mikhail frowned. "I did not know MI6 issued Glock 19X to field agents. Shorter than the 17, is better for concealment, very reliable firearm. This is a good choice."

Keeping his poker face, Bishop hid his surprise not only at the accuracy of Mikhail's assessment and his knowledge of weaponry, but also at his sudden change in demeanour. The man was trained, and trained well.

The two eyed each other across the kitchen.

Deciding they weren't getting far, Bishop thought the direct route would be best. "What interest does the SVR have in the auction?"

"What auction?"

The Russian was a fair liar, but there was enough surprise in his tone to reveal that he knew what Bishop was referring to. If only Bishop did. Mikhail's reaction when Astrid had first used the word "auction" suggested that the big man was here for the same reason the Bishop was.

Mikhail stared at Bishop. Stalemate again.

It occurred to Bishop that he could shoot out the Russian's kneecap. But besides being elementally satisfying, it was unlikely to make Mikhail talk. Plus, he'd have to clean up the blood before Temple arrived. Even worse, Temple could turn up to find a bleeding Russian on his kitchen floor. That would be somewhat difficult to explain, and not exactly the stealthy infiltration he was hoping for.

And yet…

No. He wouldn't be shooting the Russian, so they may as well talk.

Bishop tucked the pistol into his shoulder holster. His opponent raised an eyebrow but said nothing.

The MI6 agent jutted his chin. "What's with the accent?"

"I'm sorry?"

"Your accent. It's not as thick as it was yesterday. You sound less like a Cossack tractor mechanic and a little more, let's say, educated. Don't tell me you lay it on for the ladies? That's incredibly sad, my friend."

"I am not your friend." He waved a dismissive hand.

"No, I suppose not. Let's concentrate on what you *are* then, shall we? You didn't deny being in SVR. So I'm wondering what interest Russia's foreign intelligence service has in this auction. As I see it, not-friend, we have two options. Either we stay here and glare at one another until the end of time or we share intelligence to get to the bottom of the auction. What do you say?"

Mikhail's contemptuous expression lessened by about three and a half per cent, in Bishop's estimation. So he was at least considering it. Best to keep the momentum going.

"Look, it seems we're both here for the same thing, and it's not Astrid. I have a feeling you're after an arms dealer, like we are."

The words "arms dealer" made his eye twitch. He wasn't that well trained after all. Physically, perhaps, but he still had a lot to learn about covering his tells.

"What were you doing breaking into Temple's house, Mikhail?"

"I don't know who that is. I thought this was someone else's villa."

"Whose?"

"Barbara Streisand."

"I... what?"

"I am a very big fan. Huge." Mikhail's face wouldn't have been out of place at a poker tournament. "I was told this was her place and I wanted a piece of memorabilia."

Bishop's mouth dropped open. If the Russian spy thought the absurd story would throw Bishop off he was insane. Then again, if it was true, he was equally insane.

"Big Streisand fan, huh?"

"Absolutely."

"Okay, give me one Streisand album title."

Bishop really hoped the Russian was bluffing because he didn't know any himself. Streisand could have released an album called "Launching Alpacas into Space" and he wouldn't know. Bishop kind of hoped she had.

The Russian sighed, folded his arms and glared up at Bishop, then reluctantly threw up his hands. "Fine. We are looking into arms dealing."

"You're going to have to give me a little more, I'm afraid." Bishop leaned against the kitchen bench and folded his arms.

"Kali," Mikhail said. "The arms organisation we're after is called Kali."

Before Bishop could respond, a beeping emanated from Mikhail's person. His eyes darted between his chest and Bishop, as if asking for permission to reach into his jacket. The MI6 agent nodded.

Mikhail glanced at a small black device with a tiny screen. "Parameter breach. Temple is home."

Without discussion, both men scrambled towards the rope. Mikhail went first. Bishop tossed Mikhail's bag up, then his. He was careful not to grunt or show any sign of exertion as he ascended, not wanting to be shown up. When they reached the top they reeled up the rope and quietly closed the skylight behind them. Silent as ants on velvet, they scrambled along the clay tile roof and down a downpipe at the rear of the villa. Within minutes they were on the street and away. A large black Hummer sat in the driveway of Temple's estate.

Once they were sure they had no tail, both men let out an audible sigh of relief. The streets were deserted, bar the occasional stray dog who was a bit slow getting its affairs in order. Without another word, Mikhail crossed the road and walked away from Bishop.

"Where do you think you're going?" Bishop yelled after him.

Mikhail glanced back, but didn't stop. Bishop crossed the road and caught up.

The Russian glanced at Bishop and sneered. "What are you going to do, Englishman? Shoot me in the street?"

"Is there somewhere else you'd like me to shoot you?"

Mikhail gave no response as the MI6 agent matched his stride.

"Seems we're on the same team here, Mikhail."

"I work alone. I do not do teams."

Bishop hefted an eyebrow. "What's changed since last night?"

The Russian scowled, unamused. They rounded a corner and passed a restaurant. The owner tried to entice them inside, but Bishop declined with a friendly wave as they walked on.

Mikhail gave Bishop a sideways glance. "You are proposing we work together on this?"

"Maybe?" Bishop wasn't entirely sure it was a good idea. Then again, MI6's intel was sadly lacking. At the very least, MI6 could find out what SVR knew. Besides, the auction was meant to be the next day. They were running out of time. Bishop had no authority to make a deal with a foreign agency and wasn't entirely sure how receptive MI6 would be to the idea. A blunt instrument negotiating with a foreign power may send several members of his own organisation into conniptions. That was their issue. Bishop had a mission to complete, and he intended to do so in any way possible, including sidling up to an on-again, off-again enemy.

Bishop needed to determine if he could work collaboratively with the Russian. If he were honest, he thought it likely he'd squeeze the SVR agent for information and then proceed on his mission alone. It didn't seem prudent to let Mikhail know that, however.

"What do you propose," Mikhail asked, "if we do collaborate?"

"Well, the first thing we need to do, and I think you'll agree with me here, is we need hats."

"I… what?" Mikhail stared at him as if he'd gone mad.

Relishing his reaction, Bishop warmed to the idea. "You know, like, club hats."

The Russian frowned. "There will be no hats."

Bishop went on, ignoring him. "I'm thinking something like a peaked cap. Not baseball ones, obviously, more of a Breton cap. Maybe a little embroidered logo to really nail the in-a-club vibe. I'm picturing a simple black and white insignia, perhaps a spy glass or a fedora, but I'm open to suggestions."

Mikhail rolled his eyes and stomped onward. "You talk too much."

"So I've been told." Bishop gave the Russian his most charming grin. He noticed Mikhail hadn't properly wiped away the blood, which was smeared in the corner of his mouth in a crusted red stain. "What do you think, Mikhail, are we teaming up?"

The irony of the statement was not lost on Bishop, given their activities the night before.

Mikhail sighed. "I will seek guidance from my superiors." The idea didn't seem to fill him with delight. "I will advise you of their decision." He stopped walking and glared at Bishop. "Personally, I think you are an idiot and believe working with you would be like hitting my genitalia with a mallet."

"You really need to work on your trash talk there, my friend. That was like being slapped by a wet sponge cake."

"As I have said, I am not your friend."

"That much I know."

At precisely 17:00 local time, Bishop filed his report. At exactly 17:08 Paul called. "What the ruddy hell is this business about requesting to work with the Russians?"

Bishop explained the situation he'd referred to in his report, again editing out the parts pertaining to punching. As he gave his account, Paul made a series of increasingly pleased murmurs.

"How did you negotiate that?" On receiving no answer, Paul added, "How keen are the Russians?"

"Not sure, to be honest, but it's possible they'll come to the table. They're on Temple's tail as well, so that alone tells us we're onto something. If only we knew what. I'm thinking they don't want a powerful government-manip-ulating clandestine organisation swanning about desta-bilising the world any more than we do."

"What do the Russians know?"

"Undetermined. Their man was reluctant to divulge much without checking with the higher-ups." Bishop rubbed his jaw. Soft food for dinner. "Here's hoping they decide to share what they know. We may crack this case yet."

"Keep at it. We're touching base with SVR via embassy back channels; probably burning through a couple of covers in the process. If there is a way to share intel on this we may get to the auction on time. They know the clock is ticking as much as we do. Working with the *enemy* might get us to the bottom of this sooner."

Yes, Bishop thought, *sooner*. Providing Bishop with no partner or backup on this mission showed how little MI6 had thought of the assignment, and perhaps of him. Now that the Russians were on the same scent, things had changed. Bishop checked his watch. He'd wanted to check in on Astrid as soon as he'd returned to the hotel, but mission parameters dictated otherwise. Regardless, he was keen to end the conversation as soon as possible. As always, Paul seemed to have other ideas.

"There's another reason for our chat." Paul's tone was forced casual. "Five Eyes has picked up random chatter about Kali. Nothing of note, but Section 31 are chasing them up. Previously we had scant past references, and to be honest much of it came from unreliable sources. They were of such preposterous magnitude that little attention was paid, besides the obligatory report in order for the agent's expenses to be reimbursed. But…"

"But?" Bishop was wary.

"But, in light of your mission we've done some digging. Kali seems to have people scared. You were right about the retiring or missing illegal international arms dealers. Some sources are attributing the missing ones to Kali. That alone has people spooked, but there's more. Granted, it's mostly rumour, but there are some who are terrified to even utter the name. There are rumours of assassinations. Strongarming government officials. You name it. There was nothing tying any of this together, not until you uncovered it with the ambassador, then verified it with the Ruskies."

"Was that an expression of admiration, sir?" Bishop didn't care if Paul could hear him chuckle.

"Merely a statement of fact. Anything more is pure conjecture on your behalf."

"Of course. And boss?"

"Yes Bishop?"

"You're welcome."

Paul chuckled. It might also be conjecture, but Bishop believed his boss liked dealing with him because Bishop "got" his superior, and the two had formed a good bond. In their business, Bishop knew it could account for little in the end. If it were a matter of strategic importance or national security he had no doubt he'd be left flapping in the wind. The opposite was true as well. Friendship was a luxury few in espionage enjoyed.

Bishop understood why the Russians would be keen to prevent a rogue arms dealer. A new player willing to arm Chechen rebels or Ukraine dissidents would be a terrifying prospect for the current regime. They'd do all they could to stop it. As the great philosopher Kylie Minogue once said, better the devil you know.

"Oh, hang on a moment." There was rustling and muffled talk, as if Paul had placed his hand over the receiver and was talking to someone in his office. "Looks like we've got the go-ahead from the Home Office. SVR have authorised a joint mission."

"That was fast."

"British bureaucracy, the most efficient in the world, my lad." Paul's tone took on a serious edge. "I don't need to tell you to be wary of your new cohort."

"Really? The though never occurred to me."

Paul ignored the jibe. "We don't know what branch he stems from, what his background is, his specialities. I'm aware we may be lowering you into a vipers' nest. Just be careful, is all I'm saying."

"Will do, boss."

Paul tapped away on a keyboard. "Oh, and there's a note here about your man Mikhail."

"He really is a big Streisand fan?"

"No, but apparently his name isn't Mikhail at all. It's Oleg."

~

The elevator pinged and Bishop strode out. He was surprised by his own haste. He attempted to tell himself it was purely to ensure Astrid's safety. It was a lie and he knew it. Had she really taken hold of him so quickly?

She was a most unusual woman. Complex, certainly. Smart, most assuredly. Sexy, without a doubt. But she also had an alluring mix of confidence and vulnerability. It was a heady mix. Seeing her hotel room door at the end of the hall, he increased his pace.

Knocking, he waited with equal parts trepidation and anticipation. No answer. He knocked again. Silence. Once more he knocked, this time calling out, "It's me, Tyler."

The lack of response only increased his heartrate. He extracted his bump key and looked around for any witnesses. He was armed, too. Given Mikhail's—well, Oleg's—sudden appearance at Temple's villa, who knew what other forces were at work in Marrakech. Bishop wasn't taking any chances. He picked the lock and entered.

Dappled light shone through the curtains. Even in the dim room, Bishop could see enough. He drew his pistol. The place was trashed. Furniture up-ended, clothes and luggage strewn everywhere. The bed, which held such fond memories, had been overturned.

Someone had searched the room. Bishop sucked in air. There was more. Stepping into the room warily, Bishop saw pools of red on the floor. The place hadn't just been ransacked, there had been a struggle. The blood was tacky—whatever had taken place had happened at least an hour ago.

"Astrid?"

No answer.

The fact that she wasn't there and hadn't contacted him multiplied his trepidation exponentially. Bishop quickly searched the hotel room for clues, but none were immediately apparent. Every room had been tossed, cushions and pillows slashed. Without knowing what had been there to begin with, there was no way of knowing if they'd found what they sought.

MI6 had supplied a contact number for Oleg. Bishop rang it and the Russian answered. In quick order Bishop explained the situation. Oleg hung up without another word. Thirty seconds later there was a knock at the door.

Bishop let him in. "You turned up fast."

A little too fast.

The SVR agent ignored Bishop as he pushed his bulk into the room. He performed the same checks Bishop had, coming to the same conclusion. Astrid had been abducted.

For virtually the first time since he had arrived, Oleg regarded Bishop. "Who would take her?"

"I was hoping you'd tell me."

"If I knew, which I do not, why would I tell you, Englishman?"

Bishop folded his arms. "It appears our superiors want us to work together."

Oleg grunted, apparently regarding the whole idea with disdain. For the first time, Bishop noticed a haphazardly applied bandage over the back of Oleg's hand.

Nodding towards it, he asked, "Where did you get the wound?"

It was soaked red. Deep. Fresh. Bishop didn't recall any hand injury during or after their confrontation at Temple's.

Oleg glanced at the wound indifferently. "Cut it shaving."

"I see."

"How do we find Astrid?" Oleg asked with no sense of urgency.

"I have a few ideas."

He didn't, but he was working on it.

"I have told my superiors I do not like working with the United Kingdom. They did not listen." A sneer creased his face. "Your people are not to be trusted."

Bishop found the statement laughably ironic given Russia's history with the UK. "Well, be that as it may, Oleg, it is what it is. As the old saying goes, it appears the Russians are getting in bed with the English. Better get used to it."

"You think you are amusing. I do not think you are capable of being funny."

It was Bishop's turn to sneer. *You have no idea what I'm capable of, Oleg. But you'll find out soon enough.*

CHAPTER SIX

Astrid hadn't checked out of her hotel, nor had she ordered a taxi or transfer via the hotel. Bishop's various methods of persuasion combined with several fake IDs determined that she hadn't gone through the airport. The last stop was the railway station, where there was no record of her. She may have gone via road, but where? And how?

Bishop knew he was being overly hopeful. The desolation of the hotel room and the blood splashed across it meant she hadn't left voluntarily. She hadn't merely packed a bag and caught the next flight out, she'd been violently abducted.

Oleg had accompanied Bishop late into the night, though his presence was less collaborative and more like a reluctant child being dragged grocery shopping. Bishop was surprised he wasn't whining for a lollipop.

The two walked along a deserted railway platform, having hassled every official they could find. It was late, the railway station was close to deserted. The only other people about were shopkeepers closing up for the night.

They strode towards the exit, the desert breeze cooling everything after the heat of the day.

Fists deep in his pockets, Oleg grumbled, "This is a waste of time."

"Finding Astrid is a waste of time?" There was an edge to Bishop's voice. He didn't try to hide it.

"No. You said Demir advised the auction was four days away, that means tomorrow. That's what we should be concentrating on. If Kali do not wish Astrid to be found, we will not find her."

"But who is Kali?" Bishop asked. Oleg frowned and offered no reply. Bishop sighed and added, "Let me rephrase: who does SVR think Kali is?"

Reluctance swept across the Russian's face, as if he was weighing up whether to tell Bishop anything. Finally, a look of acquiescence won out. "We do not know. The fragments our intelligence organisations have discovered seem to show they are powerful. Every story is more fantastic than the next. If remotely true, we do not know how they could have achieved what they have without us knowing. The auction is the first time we have known in advance where they would be."

"And how did you know about the auction in the first place?"

The question was so loaded Bishop was surprised it didn't explode in his face. Oleg gave a boyish shrug, like a kid who had snuck into the cupboard, eaten all the birthday cake and farted on his way out.

"How did you know there was an auction, Oleg?"

Seemingly aware that a shrug would be unacceptable, the SVR agent apparently thought silence would be more satisfactory. He was wrong.

Bishop sighed. "If this partnership is going to work, we have to share intelligence. Acting all coy is neither charming nor helpful. So I suggest you stow the schoolboy routine and either start assisting or piss off back to Mother Russia. For the last time: how did you know about the auction?"

The big man gave another annoying shrug. "Let us just say you have holes in your yard."

Bishop shook his head. "I have no idea what that means."

"Holes. You have them in your yard."

"I live in an apartment."

Oleg frowned. "No. It is a meta? Meta. Yes, it is meta."

"Are you having a stroke?"

Oleg grunted. "Simile? Allegory? Whatever. A mole. You have a mole. How was it not clear?"

A mole? In MI6? That was how the Russians were here? That was concerning. Beyond concerning. Bishop doubted Oleg would be willing to supply a name, position and where they would be located on a Tuesday evening.

So many departments would have access to the Kali intel. His own, obviously. Records and Signals were used for research and verification. Department heads, their subordinates, secretaries and other functionaries. Too many and too high level to interview to any reasonable degree. Bishop would have to extract more from the big Russian over time.

"A mole, hey?" Bishop exhaled. "But MI6 hardly saw my mission as a priority. Hell, they barely considered it a mission at all. How did—"

"The word Kali triggered alerts." Oleg didn't look at Bishop, but continued to walk down the cool platform. "Once we knew of the auction, we determined we would need to be present. My organisation believe the Kali threat to be real and growing."

"You seem to know more than us," Bishop observed.

"This is a very true statement."

"On Kali."

"And all other things."

"I was talking about Kali."

"I was not."

Knowing the line of conversation would lead nowhere, Bishop decided to change tack. "What does Astrid have to do with this?"

"I do not know." He gave Bishop a sideways glance. "But if I was not interrupted by your blundering attempts to woo her last night—"

"Did you say woo?"

"—I would know much more."

Bishop frowned. "But why were you talking to Astrid in the first place?"

Groaning, as if talking further would cause him pain, Oleg replied. "I found it suspicious, a woman travelling by herself, checking in prior to the auction and checking out the day after it. I decided to question her, to ascertain if she was connected to my assignment."

"So you just find any unaccompanied woman, assume she's related to your mission and bed her?"

"Is this not what you did?"

Bishop held up a finger, then lowered it. "Let's get a taxi. It's late."

"Good. Spending time with you is like taking my sister to the prom."

Bishop puckered his brow. "Do Russians have proms?"

"Nyet."

"And do you have a sister?"

"Nyet."

"Good analogy."

They walked along the platform in silence, their foot-steps echoing into the still night. Bishop needed a shower. He was coated in a thick layer of accumulated sweat and disappointment.

Again, Bishop was perplexed by his urgent need to find Astrid. He hardly knew her. His usual modus operandi was to flee within hours of anyone he chose to sleep with. It was exceedingly uncommon for him to afford them an afterthought. Sure, she seemed to know about the auction and could be vital to the assignment, but there was more to it.

He was rather adept at making women fall in love with him, but it never occurred the other way around. It was rare for him to care, and completely unheard of during a mission. What was it about Astrid that made him break all his established rules, both personal and professional?

Meandering thoughts of Astrid brought his mind back to the discovery of her ransacked hotel room, and particularly the cut on Oleg's hand. Bishop had never intended to trust the big Russian, but the suspicious cut and his equally dubious quick arrival turned his suspi-cion into distrust, tilting towards outright disbelief.

Bishop asked again about the hand and the answer was as vague as before. The only way to get a real answer would be to utilise Temple's torture chamber. The MI6 agent wasn't unaccustomed to ruthless means of persuasion.

There was no doubt Bishop regretted believing he could trust the SVR agent. He would not make the same mistake again.

In the distance, a lone taxi sat by itself in dusty car park. A smattering of men milled about the ticket area, seemingly having nowhere to go. Bishop's thoughts wandered from the feel of Astrid's skin to how he would use Temple's torture equipment if the need arose.

They walked past a lone man in tattered pants and an Adidas t-shirt rolling a cigarette at the end of the platform. Bishop's senses were suddenly alert. The man was doing nothing more than rolling a cigarette, but it was the extra fraction of a second he took watching them pass that put Bishop on edge. That was no casual glance. They were being watched.

When they were out of earshot, Bishop whispered to Oleg, "Are you armed?"

The Russian regarded him curiously. "As a Russian, all I will say is, Без тебя бы мы никак не догадались об этом."

Bishop eyeballed him. "I don't know what that means."

"Is equivalent of, no shit Sherlock." Oleg's words dripped with sarcasm. "Yes. I am armed. Why?"

"I have a feeling our questions have aroused some local interest. I could be wrong, but be prepared."

To his credit, the big man didn't whip his head around searching for threats. His face hardened, his body tensed, and he undid the front of his jacket.

Beside the closed ticket counter two heavy-set men in jeans, t-shirts and jackets stood, doing their utmost to appear casual. They were blocking the ramp towards the exit. Their arms were folded, but not enough to hide the weaponry tucked under their jackets.

Bishop approached and nodded. "Evening, gents. Nice night for it."

The bulkier of the two stepped forward, blocking Bishop's way. He was forced to come to a halt.

The first thug frowned and gave them a sideways glance. "Nice night for what?" His accent was thick, his words fast, as if chemically enhanced. His pupils were the size of buzz-saw blades.

"Excellent question." Bishop paused. He slid his right foot backwards, defensive, ready. With a genial air, he asked, "Jenga?"

"Did you just say it is a nice night for Jenga?" It was the smaller of the two, although calling him the smaller was like calling one wrecking ball smaller than the next. His eyes were as on fire as his companion's.

Oleg kept back, one eye on the two men, another on the surrounding area, checking for further threats. Mr Roll-His-Own was further back on the platform somewhere; others could be close by. Regardless of his scepticism of moments before, Bishop was thankful for Oleg's backup. He just hoped he wouldn't get shot in the back for it.

The Russian circled behind Bishop. The two locals watched him uneasily.

"Best tell your friend to keep his distance." Thug One jutted his chin towards Oleg. "He's making me nervous."

"Why would I ask him to do that?" Bishop shrugged. "I thought we were discussing games of dexterity and physical skill? What my friend here does with his pacing is his own business." Bishop tilted his head at Thug One. "Now, are you going to let us pass, or do you have something erudite to say?"

Thug One sniffed and slipped his hand into his jacket. He had the good sense to leave it there. "I want to know where she is. You were seen with her, both of you." He nodded to Oleg. "Where is she? What did you do with the witch?"

He could only mean Astrid. So they weren't the only ones who'd noticed she was missing. Bishop decided he was playing too nice with too many people already.

"Maleficent? The Wicked Witch of the West?

Samantha from *Bewitched*? When I was a kid I had a thing for that twitch she did with her nose. Got me every time."

"We heard you were looking for her." Thug One stiffened when Oleg took a step forward. Not taking his eyes off Oleg, he continued. "You better tell us or there will be trouble."

Bishop sighed. "Not very smart, are you?"

"What… Why?"

"Do I really have to spell this out?" Bishop shook his head and gawked at Oleg.

The big Russian cracked his stern façade for the first time and issued a chortle while shaking his head. "I think these two are thicker than a whale thickshake."

Pausing for a moment, Bishop turned to Oleg, his voice low. "We really need to work on your similes. You just need to… one thing at a time."

Turning back to the thugs, Bishop let out a frustrated sigh. "Work with me here, fellas, okay? You said yourself we're looking for this 'witch'." He made air quotes with his fingers. "So why the hell are you asking what we did with her? Logic would dictate that if we did indeed have said witch, we would no longer feel the need to be searching for her in the middle of the night. It's like when people see you searching for your keys and ask if you've found them yet. Redundant, and a little idiotic. I'm terribly sorry to have stated the bleeding obvious in front of your husband here, but you left me no choice, I'm afraid."

Thug One winced and his hand delved deeper into his jacket. Oleg took another step forward and gave a warning growl. In response, Thug One removed his hand and raised his empty palm.

"That hand goes in your jacket again," Oleg sneered, "I will pound your arse."

Bishop rolled his eyes and turned to Oleg. "Look, I

feel the 'husband' thing was probably erring on the slur side of things and I'm uncomfortable with that. You telling him you're going to pound his arse isn't helping."

"I mean." Oleg motioned his fist up and down while he nodded towards the thugs.

"Again, it's unclear if you mean fisting or fighting. I don't know these gentlemen, nor do I know their particular preferences, so let's keep the innuendo to a minimum, shall we?"

"Innuendo?" Confusion creased Oleg's face. "I want to pound them."

"Are you doing this deliberately?"

Thug one coughed. "Can I interrupt?"

"I wish you would." Bishop gave Oleg a glance, as if to say, *drop it.* To his surprise, the Russian did.

"You two were last seen with the witch. She's now missing. So either you took her or you know something that can help us find her."

"And what," Bishop inspected his immaculate fingernails, "would you do with her if you found her?"

Thug One shook his head as if the question was ridiculous. "Kill her, of course."

"See? Now I'm quite unlikely to help you out."

"You don't have much of a choice." Thug Two gazed beyond Bishop and smirked.

The MI6 agent kept his eyes on the thugs, but heard Oleg turn.

"Bishop…"

Although Bishop hadn't thought it possible, Thug One's eyes grew larger. He gave a toothy grin. "You'll tell us what we want to know or you'll die slow."

"Like, old age slow?"

"Bishop…"

The MI6 agent turned to see Mr Roll-His-Own with an AK-47 slung casually over his shoulder. He wasn't alone.

Behind him, another nine scruffily dressed locals carried various weapons ranging from ragged pieces of wood to pistols that could be carbon dated back to the Second World War. The guns were tucked into waist bands, but clearly on display. A warning. Or a promise.

Glancing at Oleg, Bishop asked, "Surrender or fight?"

"Do you know Russian history at all?"

"Good lad. You want the nine or the two?"

Oleg sniffed and curled a lip towards Thug One and Thug Two. "Two. These boys need a good pounding."

"Again... look, we're going to have words later. But for now..." Bishop moved so he and Oleg were back to back, Bishop now facing the ten assailants.

Inhaling, Bishop flexed his fingers. Beyond the platform, darkness surrounded them like a heavy blanket. There seemed to be no breeze at all. The night was still. Silent.

In a lightning quick move, Bishop drew his pistol. He heard Oleg do the same. His first shot hit Roll-His-Own in the shoulder before he even raised his weapon. He went down spinning and screaming in agony. Oleg fired rapidly, anguished shrieks telling Bishop his aim was true.

Bishop's next three shots were aimed at those scrambling to pull out their pistols. Each shot found its mark and the three assailants hit the ground in quick succession. Those with planks of wood glanced at their primitive weaponry and back at Bishop. They wisely dropped their sticks and ran. Only one remained. He couldn't have been more than fifteen, nothing in his hands but a crowbar. The kid gawked at the AK-47 on the ground in front of the writhing Roll-Your-Own and then warily back at Bishop. The MI6 agent gave the kid a slow shake of his head. Thankfully, he was smart enough to get the hint. He dropped the crowbar and followed his comrades into the night.

Turning, Bishop saw Oleg standing over the thugs. Each lay on the ground, red welts in the centre of their foreheads where their lives used to be.

Walking towards him, Bishop asked, "Ever hear of witnesses?"

Oleg sighed and tucked his pistol in his shoulder holster. "Ever heard of shut your fly hole?"

"No. Mainly because it isn't a… Seriously, they need to introduce a trash talk subject at SVR. I'm happy to teach it."

Perhaps Oleg did have his uses. He had Bishop's back in a firefight. That didn't mean Bishop was prepared to trust him.

Or was he smarter than Bishop gave him credit for, and therefore more dangerous? Bishop had had his back turned when Oleg took out the thugs. Was it self-defence, or did he kill them because he had another agenda?

"What good is a witness?" Oleg shrugged. "They knew nothing of where Astrid was."

"True." Bishop jerked his head for Oleg to follow. "But they could have told us why they were so interested in her in the first place." Bishop pulled back the hammer of his pistol and held it to the head of the hyperventilating Roll-Your-Own. "Now, I'm sure this gentleman would be happy to elucidate the circumstances about which we are presently deliberating."

Roll-Your-Own was coated in dirt, his arm limp by his side, a dark red stain soaking his t-shirt. He shook his head, his eyes wide with shock and fear. "What?"

Oleg poked his good shoulder. "Tell us what you know or he'll shoot you again. Then it's my turn." Oleg aimed the gun at the man's groin.

Roll-Your-Own's eyes darted from Oleg's gun to his

happy place and back again, his sweaty features a mixture of fear and pain.

He nodded hurriedly. "Yeah, yeah, okay."

The frightened local sighed and did his best to calm himself. As he opened his mouth to speak, his head exploded in an eruption of brain and skull. The entire front portion of his face disintegrated, and his body slumped to the ground, a lifeless husk.

Bishop spun and glared at Oleg, who held up his hands and said, "Wasn't me."

The two turned their attention outward, pointing their guns at an unseen foe. In the empty distant car park—too far for a pistol—a hooded figure tossed a sniper's rifle into the back of a Citroën then jumped into the driver's seat. Within seconds, the car laid rubber onto the highway and was gone.

Bishop and Oleg stood alone in the night, surrounded by death and silence. Without uttering a word, the two strode towards the exit. Nothing further could be discovered here.

Why hadn't the sniper taken them out? Why spare them? It curdled Bishop's brain trying to make sense of it.

A lone taxi they'd seen before sat at the rank. The driver sat reclining in his seat, listening to some dreadful R & B song at a ridiculous volume, apparently unaware that a gunfight had played out 50 metres away. They engaged his services and drove away. No one followed.

Left to his own thoughts, Bishop ran through the events in his mind. He could have sworn the distant sniper who took out Roll-Your-Own looked familiar. Granted, he'd been upside down and bleeding at the time, but the hooded figure he'd just seen appeared remarkably similar to the one who'd stared him down at Lambert Estate. The assassin who had killed Demir.

Bishop had vowed revenge on those who had killed

the police and the ambassador; now the catalyst for that vengeance was in Marrakech.

As the taxi drove into the night, Bishop swore one thing. In the next twenty-four hours retribution would be his, no matter the cost.

CHAPTER SEVEN

When the taxi arrived at the hotel, Oleg exited and strode inside, leaving Bishop to pay. Bishop was so happy to be rid of the Russian, he didn't even mind. He was decidedly undecided on the Russian.

On arriving in his hotel room, Bishop ordered a bottle of scotch from room service and took a shower. For the next three hours he scrutinised the day's camera footage from Temple's villa. And drank.

Other forces were after Astrid. The assumption was that it was all tied to the auction somehow. But how? Why? What or whom did she represent? How was she involved? The brief coded conversation they'd had in her hotel room had suggested she was involved reluctantly. Was that true? Why had the thugs referred to her as a witch? Why were they after her in particular? Who had kidnapped her in the first place?

So many questions. No apparent answers.

Bishop decided to focus on what he could control. Like a sick voyeur, Bishop watched Temple plod around his home. The man seemed elementally plain, pottering around in various rooms, performing the most mundane tasks. Unpacking and washing clothes, tidying, cleaning benchtops. No untoward behaviour. No suspicious activity. No Astrid.

The man himself seemed equally unremarkable. He was in his mid-thirties—younger than Bishop had anticipated. Bishop had envisioned a dumpy, middle-aged man. In reality, Temple had a strong jaw, dark curly hair and an intelligent face. He was like a good-looking accountant, a level of attractiveness where the bar was set low.

Watching the footage, Bishop wondered if the man was worthy of surveillance at all. He saw him make a sandwich, watch a football match and put himself to bed. Hardly supervillain territory, but first impressions were always fraught.

The footage of Temple going to bed seemed like a cue for Bishop. His bleary eyes demanded respite and he allowed himself a few short hours' rest. His sleep was interrupted by tormented dreams of a tortured Astrid, her perfect body sliced and defiled. The piercing morning sun was a welcome interruption.

Knocking the empty bottle of Laphroaig off the sheet-tangled bed, Bishop tried to focus on the laptop screen. It was a live feed. It took a few seconds for his eyes to adjust, but when they did, Bishop sat upright. Temple was readying himself to leave the villa. A backpack was on the kitchen table, and he was eating the last of his toast.

Bishop picked up his phone, unlocked the screen and stared at it until it locked again. Did he want Oleg's help? Sure, he'd been helpful the night before, but did Bishop trust him? The answer was an emphatic no. Strategically, should he involve Oleg? That was another question entirely.

The auction was scheduled for today; he did not have

the luxury of finding nice people to work with. The Russians seemed to have more information about Kali than MI6, and they may well need it before the mission was through. Then there was the subject of the mole. SVR would never divulge who had supplied the information, but perhaps Oleg would let slip a tiny sliver of a clue that would help them narrow the search.

As Temple bit into the final piece of toast, Bishop bit into his pride. Mission parameters took precedence. He called Oleg.

Two minutes later, Bishop stood over Oleg at a table in the dining room.

"Temple's about to leave. We need to follow him."

Before the Russian was a sickening pile of bacon, fried eggs and sausages, all coated in a slick layer of grease. It was a far cry from Bishop's daily routine of green juice and two hundred push-ups.

"The auction's today, we have to go."

"But I am hungry."

"That stuff will clog your arteries." Bishop looked at the pools of oil on the plate. "I'm doing you a favour."

"Napoleon said an army marches on its stomach."

"First of all, a Russian should never quote Napoleon. Second, I don't plan on marching. Third, I'm leaving right now, so either you come with me or this thing is over before it begins. Your choice."

The big man stood, gave his food a longing glance and left the table. A minute later they were in a taxi.

The short trip to Temple's neighbourhood was conducted in silence, apart from the growling of Oleg's stomach. Bishop watched the live feed from the villa on his mobile. Temple seemed unhurried as always.

Bishop advised the driver to pull up a block from the villa. The streets were quiet. Stray dogs continued their morning routine.

Without turning, the taxi driver said, "Twenty dirham, gentlemen."

Bishop leaned forward. "May I ask your name?"

The young, dark-skinned woman turned and issued a broad smile. She appeared barely old enough to see over the dash. She took a moment to think. "Janet."

Bishop chuckled. "Okay, but what is your real name, not the one you use for stupid Western tourists?"

Her smile stayed in place. "Zoya."

"May I ask, Zoya, what you normally make in a day? Please feel free to inflate the figure for the sake of negotiation."

"Perhaps four or five hundred dirham, sayyid."

Bishop whistled, then, seeing Zoya's expression of concern that she'd priced herself out of the market, he winked. "We'll give you four thousand dirham to be our personal driver today. Take us where we need to go, wait when we need. It could be dangerous, it could be boring. What do you say?"

Her pleased face lapsed into wariness. "No funny business?"

"No funny business. This is purely a transportation arrangement, I assure you."

The young woman nodded. "For two thousand dirham I would change my real name to Jeff."

"Good lass." Bishop stuffed a wad of currency in her hand. "A down payment. Wait here and we'll be back soon enough. Okay?"

Zoya nodded as she counted the notes.

The two spies exited the taxi and walked the rest of the way on foot.

"Can she be trusted?" Oleg asked.

Bishop eyed his companion. "As much as the next person."

For ten minutes, the two stood in silence, waiting for

Temple to emerge. When he finally did, the supposed auctioneer strode towards his Humvee and started the penis-compensation masquerading as a car.

As the automatic gates of the villa vibrated open, Bishop and Oleg trotted back to the taxi and jumped in the back.

"Zoya, do you watch a lot of movies?" Bishop asked as the Humvee slowly drove out of the driveway. "Because I want you to follow that car."

"Yes, sayyid! It will be like *Driving Miss Daisy*!"

Bishop shook his head. "It's nothing like *Driving Miss Daisy*."

"It's almost exactly like the movie!"

"You and I have very different recollections of *Driving Miss Daisy*."

Motioning to the Humvee, Oleg said, "Can we please…"

They took off. Within minutes it became clear that Zoya was a natural surveillance officer. Without being asked, she hung back far enough to avoid drawing attention, but close enough that she never lost sight of Temple's car. Occasionally she'd put on a hat or sunglasses to mix up her appearance, in case anyone was watching. She was smart and had natural instincts. Bishop would be sure to pass on the kid's details to MI6 in case they ever needed an asset on the ground.

For the next twenty minutes the three followed Temple's every move. He drove his car at a leisurely pace, considerately allowing cars in at intersections, and appeared to be in no hurry whatsoever. Hardly the actions of an arms dealer about to host a world-shaking auction.

In a remarkably downmarket part of town, the big car double-parked in front of an equally downmarket second-hand store. Rickety tables on the footpath overflowed with faded, broken goods. Old household appliances, cheap toys, mismatched crockery. Bishop hoped the auction wasn't to take place here. He didn't relish the idea of returning to MI6 and advising he'd got a really good deal on a broken toaster.

From 40 metres away, Bishop watched Temple pick up a pair of penguin-shaped salt and pepper shakers at random, hand over a couple of dirty notes and jump back in his Humvee. Oleg and Bishop exchanged confused expressions.

Two more stores were visited, and equally random goods were purchased. A chipped decorative bowl and child's doll that was missing an arm. His motives weren't any clearer. Bishop had seen Temple's house, none of these items went with his décor. Unless he was changing his style to bohemian homeless chic.

At the next decrepit store he stopped at, Temple headed inside. Bishop asked Zoya to follow him in and observe from afar, emphasising that under no circumstances should she engage the target. She gave a salute and practically ran in, relishing her new undercover role.

After a few minutes their impromptu spy emerged with her regular beam, white teeth glistening. "He wandered around and bought a… there," Zoya pointed at Temple walking towards his Humvee.

In his hands, he carried a bedside lamp with a tatty pink lampshade.

Zoya nodded in the man's direction. "Five dirhams. He hardly bartered, he is not a good purchaser of goods." When she saw the men's blank expressions she added, "My name is Zoya." Her face was enveloped by teeth and gums. "It means bargain, so I would know."

Bishop nodded, but his mind was elsewhere. That was roughly fifty pence. Why would a man who lives in a villa and drives an expensive foreign car go around buying useless lamps and other pointless crap? Was he going to sell them on eBay? Was he hard up for cash?

Addressing Oleg, he asked, "Do you know what is going on?"

The big man shrugged. "I do not know. This makes as much sense as why the English believe dogs bollocks is a good thing. Or your love of cricket. Or Marmite. Many things do not make sense."

"Thank you for your input, Oleg. Invaluable as always."

They continued to follow Temple's car, but he didn't visit any more stores. In fact, his meandering driving seemed to abate; he became more deliberate. Like he had somewhere to be.

More time passed and the concentration of buildings lessened. He was heading out of town. Eventually high-density housing gave way to suburbs, suburbs gave way to shacks, shacks gave way to stretches of desert. Soon they needed to give Temple's car a lot more distance, as they were the only two cars on the stretch of highway. The warm sun and the thrum of the taxi's tyres on the bitumen lulled Bishop into a daze.

"Will he drive all day?" Zoya asked, breaking the monotony. "I do not wish to be pulled over by the police at night."

"Why would they do that?"

Zoya kept her eyes on the road. "I only have one working headlight."

"Will they take your taxi licence away?"

"What makes you think I have a licence?" Zoya let loose a madwoman's cackle and remained amused for some time, despite her companions' silence.

"He's turning."

Zoya's words shook Bishop from his stupor. The big black car turned, but there was no road. Amid low sand dunes, the Humvee ploughed through and over small mounds. It was as if he had suddenly become bored with driving along roads and wanted to try something different. Or discovered he had a tail.

The road, if it could be called that, was rocky but relatively flat. They waited until Temple was out of view and drove slowly, ensuring they were well out of sight. They followed for roughly a kilometre, until they caught sight of the rear of the car behind a dune. It was a hundred metres away. Temple couldn't have seen them, but if they proceeded further they would be spotted.

"Pull over," Bishop said. "Turn around and go behind that dune." It would hide the taxi if Temple doubled back. "Be ready to floor it when needed. We'll climb the dune and see where he's headed."

"We will?" The Russian seemed unimpressed.

Bishop rolled his eyes. "Afraid of getting sand in your panties?"

"Quite frankly, yes."

In spite of the bitching, Oleg came with Bishop and the two scrambled up the nearest dune. The black car had pulled up in front of a large white domed tent. A fancy one at that. The Arabian style wouldn't have been out of place in a Tony Curtis movie.

The area was surprisingly flat and sand-free. You could drive from the road without much trouble if you knew where to go. As there was nothing else nearby, Bishop had the impression the tent was temporary. The surrounding high dunes gave perfect cover.

The two spies ducked down as Temple emerged from the tent empty-handed. He slid behind the wheel of the Humvee.

In a low voice, Bishop spoke to Oleg while keeping an eye on the approaching car. "You go with Zoya. If Temple goes back to the villa, wait until he's settled, then come back for me."

"Why, what will you do?" He eyed Bishop suspiciously.

"I'm going to find out what's in the tent." The gap was narrowing. In seconds Bishop would miss his chance.

"And take all the credit for the British Empire? I do not like this plan."

"Hate to break it to you, but there is no Empire. Hasn't been for a good number of years. Two choices, Oleg: we're in this together or not at all. You have three seconds."

The big Russian eyed the approaching car and growled. "Fine, but if you—"

Bishop didn't wait for the rest of the sentence. He rounded the dune to stay out of sight. It forced Oleg to rush back to the taxi, their directives clear. The SVR agent was wary that Bishop wanted to search the tent alone. He was right to be.

As a child, Bishop never liked to play with others, preferring to have all the toys to himself. Little had changed, although these days the toys were a little more interesting.

Bishop watched the Russian scramble down the dune, sending cascades of sand flowing after him. The Humvee turned slowly towards the highway, going back the way they'd come. The taxi followed several seconds later, keeping its distance.

Safe in the knowledge that Temple was far away, and Oleg too, Bishop braved the descent. The massive tent was surrounded on all sides by sand dunes; no one would know it was there unless they had explicit instructions. It was well hidden. But why?

Approaching the tent, Bishop did his best to sound

like an incompetent tourist. "Hello? I've broken down. Can anyone call a tow truck?"

Bishop hoped no one would take him up on the request. He no longer had a car. Luckily enough, no one answered. The place seemed deserted.

Opening one of the flaps, Bishop stepped inside. The interior was decked out like a luxury Bedouin tent, or at least a Hollywood version of one. With lush carpets and elegant Moroccan ceiling lights, if it was meant to create a sense of old-world elegance it only half succeeded. Two dozen folding chairs faced a podium. On the podium sat a lectern and two more folding seats, noticeably fancier than the rest.

Sitting on the podium was a large cardboard box. Bishop flipped it open. Inside were the odds and ends Temple had collected. The penguin salt and pepper shakers, the lamp, all of it. Picking them up one by one, Bishop inspected them but found nothing of interest. No hidden compartments for microfilm—not that anyone went in for that sort of thing anymore, but still…

What the hell is this all about?

Next to the box was another, less weathered one. Bishop opened that too. Inside were paddles, each labelled with a unique number.

They'd found it. This was the auction. This was where it would take place. Finally, they would have answers. Finally, Bishop would have revenge.

CHAPTER EIGHT

The few devices left over from Temple's house surveillance came in handy. In quick succession, Bishop planted visual and listening devices so they could observe and record all goings-on in the tent. He still had no idea what the auction was for, who was attending or how it was meant to work. It was unlikely that a crate of rocket launchers would be rolled out and men in wax moustaches would bid between maniacal laughs. Although right now it seemed that anything was possible.

Demir had risked everything, his career, his life, to get a seat at the auction. Kali were ruthless, willing to murder ambassadors in police custody. They were not to be underestimated. As he silently left the tent, a feeling of relief enveloped Bishop. The sensation annoyed him. He should feel no relief. Not yet. There was much to do before he could rest. There were people to rescue.

Astrid had disappeared due to the auction. That alone sped Bishop's movements. Finding the auction site meant he was closer to the truth, although it didn't feel like it.

Oleg called to advise that Temple had returned to his

villa and had remained there for half an hour. Bishop was well away from the tent, already planning the next few hours. They would regroup, arm themselves and prepare. The auction was to take place tonight, they had to be ready.

Zoya's taxi arrived twenty minutes later. She dropped Bishop and Oleg at the hotel, where they split off to their respective rooms. Zoya went to fuel up the taxi and catch some sleep before she was needed again.

After filing his report, Bishop readied himself. Changing into his suit, he checked his two pistols, sniper rifle, four spare magazines and surveillance equipment. His monitoring devices showed Temple wandering around his home, doing nothing in particular, just pottering. No one had returned to the auction site, but it would only be a matter of time.

Milling about in the lobby awaiting Oleg, Bishop eyed every passer-by. He tugged at the cuff of his slim-fitting blue tuxedo. Since the run-in with the thugs at the train station, he assessed anyone as a potential enemy. It was unknown what factions were at play, what was really going on. One thing was certain: Bishop was determined to find out.

With the graceless cadence of a lumberjack, Oleg approached. The lumberjack comparison was apt; he seemed to be dressed as one. He wore sturdy worker boots, black jeans and a dark flannel shirt so worn it would make a third-year university student think twice.

"What in the name of Gorbachev's birthmark are you wearing, man? You seem dressed for wrestling bears, not espionage."

Oleg looked Bishop up and down and sneered. "Are we going to the opera?"

"Well, we aren't going to Uncle Steve's barbecue and hoedown." Bishop inhaled, trying to quell his astonishment. "What if you're discovered? You going to tell them you're on your way to a Nirvana concert?"

"No, I will tell them I am a construction worker on leave before a construction conference. What about you, what's your cover? You were on your way to a performance of Madame Butterfly and got lost?"

There was no use arguing. Given the palatial surrounds of the auction tent, it seemed obvious the participants would be equally well adorned. There was no way someone who looked like a scruffy, unemployed bum would be invited to an international arms deal, or whatever the auction was. A spy was meant to blend in with their surrounds; Oleg never would. If they were attending a five-star resort, Oleg would be the turd in the swimming pool. The thought amused Bishop all the way out of town.

Zoya dropped Oleg off first. She slowed the taxi and he hit the ground running, sniper rifle strapped to his back. He disappeared into the dunes 1 kilometre south of the tent, his mission parameters clear: he was backup. Bishop would observe the auction from afar through his video feed. Oleg would step in if things went wrong.

When Zoya dropped Bishop off north of the tent he gave her double the agreed fee and told her not to stay close by or take risks. He or Oleg would call if needed, but Bishop made her promise she would stay far away. She was a sweet, smart young girl, and he didn't want her to come to any harm. He waved her goodbye and trudged into the desert.

Half an hour later, he was in position. Like Oleg, he dug a hole and set up his low-profile reinforced camouflaged tent, covered in sand to ensure it blended in perfectly with his surrounds. Next, he unpacked his rifle to view the outside of the tent, then positioned his mobile phone beside him so he could observe the goings-on inside. He checked the time. It would be a long wait until nightfall.

Once Bishop had performed a quick comms check with Oleg there was nothing to do but wait. Thankfully, the day was cool, but that didn't mean Bishop wasn't sweating. He opened a ration pack and chowed down on the cardboard-like substance. He'd learned in the army to eat when you could, because you had no idea when your next meal would come.

"You sound like a cow eating tinfoil."

Bishop baulked. He realised Oleg was speaking to him via his headset.

"Sorry, forgot to switch the mic off."

"Just as well. I would have been angry if I thought you were deliberately eating at me."

It would be a long wait. Bishop decided they may as well use the time. "What are you shooting with, Oleg?

"OSV-96."

An excellent sniper rifle. Amazing range. Of course, it was Russian.

"And what are you using, Englishman?"

"Accuracy International AXMC."

"Pah. My weapon has a range of two and a half kilometres. Yours is, what? Half that?"

"A bit more, but reliable as hell."

"As reliable as anything from United Kingdom."

"That's what I said."

"It was not meant as a compliment."

"Oh, I know."

Oleg grunted. "Russian is better. Always better."

Through his scope, Bishop could barely make out the lump where Oleg was camouflaged. Someone could be standing right next to him and Bishop wouldn't know. He peered through the scope. He could take out Oleg if he wanted, theoretically. The range was beyond the limits of his weapon, but that didn't prevent Bishop's finger momentarily twitching on the trigger. He had no doubt that two kilometres away, the Russian was thinking the same.

Not knowing how to respond, Bishop chuckled. There was a piece of information he needed and the only way to find out was to keep the Russian talking. "Oleg, where are you from?"

"Are we dating now?" The SVR agent tutted. "Next you will be asking my top five movies and what is my favourite Pokémon."

He was right, Bishop didn't care. There was no need for civility. But that wasn't why he'd asked.

"I won't tell you," Oleg said matter-of-factly.

"Tell me what?"

"About the mole. Do not try and put butter up me."

"Put butter where?"

"I will not tell you, Bishop. This is for you and the rest of your MI6 blunderers to figure out on your own."

At least he was smart enough to know why Bishop was even talking to him. There was no doubt MI6 would be concerned about leaked information. There would surely be investigations already underway in light of what Oleg had previously said.

There was another option, however. Maybe there was no mole at all. The Russians could have intercepted a message, or there could be a hundred other possibilities. Oleg's mention of a mole could have been planted so MI6 would tear itself apart. That would be a callous and unscrupulous move. If that was what Oleg had done, Bishop couldn't help but be impressed.

They lapsed into silence. For two hours, nothing happened, besides sweat finding new and exciting places to invade. The tent remained empty, the sun beat down, the wind refused to blow. Darkness dropped like an anvil. Finally, a van drove through the dunes, and people in crisp white uniforms climbed out. The caterers had arrived. Soon after, slightly better-dressed staff appeared carrying tubs of ice. Bar staff. Then others arrived, more heavily armed. Security. About a dozen. Chatter was at a minimum, their focus absolute. They were well trained.

Oleg and Bishop kept chatter to a minimum, preferring to keep an eye on the surrounds. That soon became a full-time operation. Temple turned up in his penis-compensating vehicle, issuing orders and generally being unpleasant. Not long after, it seemed as if every mode of transport imaginable made an appearance. Big luxury cars, more practical dune buggies, what appeared to be a snowmobile, even a hovercraft. Virtually everything but a camel train.

The guests were dressed immaculately in tuxedos and fine dresses. No one appeared to be under fifty.

"They're all very well dressed, wouldn't you say, Oleg? Not a lumberjack to be seen."

"You are not as amusing as you think." Oleg let out a sigh. "I wish I could come inside the tent."

"What?"

"The tent, I wish I could come in it."

Bishop stifled a cough. "Please don't use 'come' in that context again."

"Why not?"

"Look, I know you don't understand some of the subtleties of the English language, but there are some contexts in which you just don't use the word 'come'. Trust me, okay?"

"I do not understand. Why can't I come if I want to, Bishop?"

"You need to stop talking."

Before the Russian could respond, the loud *whop whop whop* of helicopter rotor blades filled the air. Over a distant dune, a silver Airbus H155 floated into view. A ten-million-dollar ride. These folks certainly weren't holding out their hands for welfare. As sand flew in all directions, well-to-dos scurried for the protection of the tent and shielded their eyes from the sandstorm. Someone was making a grand entrance.

As the helicopter slowed for landing, it looked increasingly likely that it was going to land on Oleg's position. *Right* on his position. Bishop wanted to issue a warning, but it would be fruitless. First of all, Oleg wouldn't be able to hear him, and secondly, he was probably more concerned with a helicopter landing on his head at that precise moment of time.

The Airbus landed smoothly in a whirl of sound and fury. The rotors slowed and two men strode out, ducking low. Bishop suspected the landing skids had touched down either side of Oleg's hiding place. But it was so far away, and the chopper had dispersed so much sand, it was impossible to know.

Once the men were clear, one in a suit and one in a Middle-Eastern thobe, the rotors sped up and the helicopter took off, leaving a sandstorm and deafening silence in its wake.

Bishop waited several moments. "You alive, Oleg?"

No answer. He asked again. Silence.

Had Oleg been crushed to death? A five-ton helicopter landing on you would put a crimp in anyone's day.

Bishop could carry on the mission alone, but it would be a hell of a lot tougher. He didn't trust Oleg, but they seemed to be on the same team, at least temporarily. Bishop's thoughts turned to how he would proceed solo. It was, after all, how he'd started this mission, and it appeared it would be how he ended it.

There was a grunt over Bishop's earpiece. "That was not pleasant."

"You alright, Oleg?"

"I feel like a very large woman just made love to me. Without permission."

"So it didn't land on you then?"

"Almost. The skids landed each side. One metre either way and I would have been as flat as a British Eurovision entry."

"That would probably be amusing if I knew anything about Eurovision." Bishop peered through his sniper scope. "Did you see who got out of the chopper?"

"Surprisingly, no. I was too busy getting my anus sandblasted."

"I may be wrong, but I could have sworn the Saudi Finance Minister just flew in."

"Essam bin Faisal is here?"

"I believe so."

The Saudi minister was infamous for whipping not one, but two servants to death. The fact that he retained his position demonstrated the power he held.

Bishop scratched the back of his head. "And you saw who got out of the Bentley before? He had the stunning brunette on his arm."

"I was concentrating on the brunette."

"The Pakistani Minister of Defence."

Abas Khloro had been causing rumblings for some time, making it plain he disapproved of the popular Pakistani president. Many believed a coup d'état was in the wind.

"What is this, Oleg? The Legion of Doom?"

"I don't know."

Bishop watched the screen showing the interior of the tent. There were around twenty-five guests in total, forming a melange of headdresses, skin colours, formal dress and uniforms. Booze flowed, waiters and waitresses carried silver plates of hors d'oeuvres. It seemed pleasant enough, like a congenial get-together, except people had died to keep it secret.

New arrivals slowed to a trickle. By eight, everyone appeared to have arrived. Bishop thought it was telling. These were obviously important people, wealthy leaders in their field, yet each and every one of them was afraid to turn up late. Very telling indeed.

On the platform, Temple rang a tiny bell. Every head turned.

"Ladies and gentlemen." He spoke with a heavy French accent. "Please take your seats, we shall start the auction."

Temple wasn't one for foreplay, clearly. When all the guests had taken their seats, the Frenchman took his position behind the lectern.

"Lot one."

As Temple spoke the words, a young woman who could have strutted down any catwalk in Paris sashayed forward. In her hands was a red velvet cushion; on it, the two penguin-shaped salt and pepper shakers. The cheap gaudy trinkets were accorded so much reverence Bishop nearly smiled. Nearly.

"Starting bid," Temple lifted an expectant eyebrow, "ten million American dollars."

Bishop knew inflation was a problem but that was ridiculous.

"Did he say ten *million* dollars?" Oleg was as stunned as he was.

The paddles Bishop had seen on his earlier reconnoitre began flying into the air. Bidding was furious. In no time at all the price was over fifty million. Then eighty. It finally tapped out at ninety-seven million, three hundred thousand.

"Sold!" Temple rapped his gavel on the lectern. "Compliments to Mr bin Faisal!"

The Saudi Minister's fellow guests patted him on the back. He had paid nearly a hundred million for a pair of penguin salt and pepper shakers that had been purchased earlier in the day for a few cents. The amazing thing was, he seemed quite pleased with himself. Bishop had to wonder why they were congratulating him. Essam bin Faisal seemed to be the worst finance minister in the history of the world.

Soon the crowd was back at it. The second lot was the tattered doll with the missing arm. That went for three hundred million, five hundred thousand. It was purchased by the Pakistani Minister of Defence.

"This is absurd," Oleg spat. "Why are these people purchasing junk for these prices? I once saw comic book sell for three million dollars. I can go down shop and the buy same comic for—"

"Oleg, shut up."

"What did you—"

"You've got company. Three o'clock."

Through his scope, Bishop saw two figures approaching Oleg's position in the dark. They weren't performing a routine patrol; they stalked towards him in a direct line, as if they knew he was there. Had the pilot seen something when he landed?

"Two figures, full webbing, earpieces. FN P90 submachine guns, multiple sidearms. They're not here to issue parking tickets. You have thirty seconds."

In a low voice, Oleg growled, "Received."

Headlights illuminated the exterior of the tent. A heavy looking black Mercedes SUV pulled up, sitting deep on its suspension, likely armoured. Through the scope of his sniper rifle, Bishop saw two figures emerge from the vehicle. One was a bulky man with close-cropped hair who carried himself with the discipline of a soldier. A scar ran diagonally across his forehead above a red bushy beard. He spoke hurriedly into his headset. When he saw the second passenger, Bishop's mouth dropped open.

He knew the second figure. Well, not personally, but he certainly knew him on sight. It was the same hooded individual who had assassinated Roll-Your-Own at the railway station, who had stalked and likely killed Astrid. The same person who had assassinated Demir. And the very same son of a bitch who had nearly done the equivalent to Bishop when he was upside down and bleeding in his car. His finger caressed the trigger.

"Status?"

Oleg's harsh hiss brought Bishop back to the crisis at hand. He repositioned his rifle sight.

"Twenty metres. They're heading straight for you, you've been made."

"Take the shot. I'll deal with the leftovers."

The request was problematic for all sorts of reasons. The first was range. Oleg and Bishop had positioned themselves within reach of the tent, not each other. Oleg was roughly double the recommended range of his AXMC. Even the superior reach of the Russian's OSV sniper rifle would have a hard time at that distance.

The second reason was one of logistics. As soon as Bishop fired, whether his aim was true or not, they'd be made. Security would scour the landscape for any trace of them. Currently they were a potential threat. An academic idea. After the first shot they would become enemy combatants and would be hunted down.

The third reason was simple enough. He despised and distrusted the Russian. Did he want to die for the SVR agent? No. Bishop wasn't even sure he wanted to miss lunch for him. Then again, if the roles were reversed,

Bishop would hope the big Russian, for all his misgivings, would have his back. Would he though? The MI6 agent wouldn't bet his life on it.

Bishop swung the scope back to the tent. Red Beard was there, standing erect at the entrance. Judging by the way he carried himself, he definitely had to be ex-military. The arrogance in his stance suggested he'd been an officer. The hooded assassin was gone. Bishop couldn't decide what was more worrying, the fact that he'd missed his chance or that the assassin could be anywhere. Bishop decided on the latter. It was like trying to capture a spider in your bedroom at night and missing your chance, only to have it scuttle away. A missing spider was far more worrying than one right in front of you.

"What are you waiting for, *Englishman*, a spatula?"

"If you'd shut up I could concentrate, *Ruskie*."

As Bishop repositioned his rifle, the two figures slowed their approach. The lead guard aimed two fingers precisely at where Oleg was hidden.

Drawing on his SAS experience, Bishop slowed his breathing, calculated the distance, the terrain, the wind speed and direction. At this range it was like trying to shoot an arrow between the eyes of a hummingbird. In a hurricane. While riding a horse. Even if his aim was true, they would be discovered immediately. Everything he'd done to uncover the auction would be for nothing. Was the Russian worth all that?

Deathly still, Bishop watched the figures circle behind Oleg. He would be dead within seconds.

Fuck it.

Bishop took the shot. The result wasn't instantaneous; the bullet had to travel over 2 kilometres. Around five seconds later the lead figure spun around. He fired his pistol harmlessly into the air as he tumbled backwards, sliding down the sand. Before Bishop could reposition his second shot, Oleg was up and firing. The second figure was dead before he hit the ground.

Oleg trudged to where the first attacker had fallen. Two more pistol shots assured the kill. The big Russian sighed. "That was some shooting. I do not know many soldiers alive who could have taken that shot."

"A compliment?"

"An observation."

Bishop sighed. "You better bug out, they'll be on you in seconds."

"*We* better bug out. There is nothing more we can do here. Not even a fancy tuxedo will help you."

He was right. They were blown. The dunes would be crawling with security in minutes. As well hidden as Bishop was, there was no guarantee he would remain so. His scope zeroed in on the tent. Red Beard was screaming into a walkie-talkie and pointing into the night. Inside, people were half out of their seats, and some of the guests were pointing and shouting. Bishop unmuted the feed.

"Ladies and gentlemen!" Temple raised his palms, trying to calm the crowd. "Everything is under control, I assure you. A mere skirmish. Please remain calm. There are four more lots to be sold tonight, and you do not want to come all this way to miss out. Do not forget the next lot is our exquisite ornamental lamp. The shipment must be picked up this week, no exceptions. You mustn't miss out." That seemed to quell the crowd, and they sat once more. "Believe me, ladies and gentlemen, we shall have the two troublemakers apprehended in no time."

Two.

It was time to bug out.

Ensuring all his accumulated data and footage had been uploaded to the satellite, Bishop set a timed charge to detonate in five minutes. All trace of his hideout would soon be eradicated. If Red Beard or his cohorts happened to stumble upon his hideout in around four or so minutes' time, they would be equally eradicated.

The last image Bishop saw of the auction was the Saudi Minister for Finance being congratulated for winning another lot. He was on a roll.

Squeezing out of his sand-covered hiding place, Bishop strapped on his sniper rifle and ran. The plan was for Oleg to head south, Bishop north, to the highway they had turned off.

Over the headset, Bishop asked, "Position update?"

"Point five kilometres south of original. Making good headway. No tail that I can identify."

That put him roughly 2 kilometres away, on foot. He would be no help if Bishop ran into trouble.

"Copy. Heading towards highway. ETA for rendezvous, one hour. Mark. Over. Out."

After clearing the first dune, no light could be seen from the tent. A quarter moon hung in the sky, the only source of illumination. Bishop was fit, some would say overly so, but he heaved at the exertion. Sprinting on sand was problematic. You expend a lot of effort while making little headway. Bishop had slogged over two sandbanks and felt like he'd run a half marathon.

There was also something else about dunes. They made it difficult to mask your footfalls. On the dune in front of Bishop, a series of footsteps had disturbed the sand and created mini avalanches with every step. Someone had been this way, and recently. The sand was still falling.

From all around, Bishop heard raised voices. There were at least three, possibly more. Voices carried in the cold desert air—they could be 10 metres away or a hundred. Taking down one assailant was fine. Two, doable. Three, again, doable, but prone to the other side lucking out. Bishop had no desire to offer the other side any chance of good fortune.

Unslinging the sniper rifle from his back, Bishop tossed it on the ground and covered it in sand. Better to happen across an enemy without a plainly obvious weapon. Plus, it was good for long range, not close quarters. He had two pistols tucked into the back of his pants for that.

The voices seemed closer now, more urgent. They spoke English, but their words were nonsensical.

"Charlie, at the crest, copy Panda."

"Cross gain, Artemis covering."

Code. It meant something to someone. Either that or he was overhearing a Scrabble match between an illiterate and an idiot.

"Hold it!"

Bishop turned to see Red Beard atop a dune, aiming a pistol directly at him. Instead of going for his pistol, he threw his hands in the air in frustration.

"Oh, thank fucking Christ! I've been wandering around this godforsaken place for hours." Bishop lowered his hands and his tone, tugging at the lapels of his tux. "I'm terribly sorry, I seem to have gotten lost. I'm looking for a large white tent and an auction."

"It's already started." Red Beard's voice was low and even, his accent American, Midwestern. He mumbled incomprehensibly into his walkie-talkie. "I thought all guests had arrived."

"I assure you that is far from the case. My… employer would be most upset with me if I didn't procure some… let's say, essential items. Now, if you could point me in the right direction, I have little time and an itchy chequebook." Bishop's tone dripped with arrogance. He assumed any invitee to the auction would be disinclined to speak to underlings.

Red Beard's eyes narrowed. "Wouldn't happen to have an invite on you by any chance?"

There was shuffling behind the spy. Red Beard's backup had arrived. His posture became more upright. He was relaxed. The ex-soldier lowered his weapon and thrust it into his hip holster. Bishop was surprised he didn't spin it first, like they did in westerns. He must be getting soft in his old age. Even with backup—Bishop assumed two—you never relinquish your weapon in front of a likely foe. It would be Red Beard's last mistake.

"I did, but wouldn't you know it, I seem to have misplaced it with all this scurrying about. I believe I'll have a word with Temple when this is all over. An auction in the desert is all very clandestine and whatnot, but parking is a bitch and frankly, the lack of a decent bar is criminal."

The sound of sliding footsteps meant those behind were closing in. Making their way down the hill, they approached slowly. That would be *their* last mistake.

Red Beard sighed. "Let's cut the crap, shall we? You're no more a guest than I am. You're at the bottom of a sand dune, surrounded. What do you expect to happen?"

Bishop tilted his head. "Is a back rub out of the question?"

"It is." Red Beard folded his arms.

"I see." Bishop scratched the back of his neck. "How about a lift to the nearest bar? I could murder a pina colada."

To Bishop's surprise, Red Beard laughed. "You've got balls, I'll give you that much. Not that it matters." He nodded to the men behind him. "Temple has ways with the likes of you."

"So I've heard."

"What's your name?"

"Let me write it down for you."

When Bishop reached into his pocket Red Beard flinched, but relaxed when he slowly pulled a pen from his jacket.

The spy considered the pen reverently. "You see, I've learned there's absolutely one thing you should never ever do when apprehending a suspect."

Bishop clicked the pen and tossed it high into the air. All eyes followed the white object. Pivoting one hundred and eighty degrees, Bishop threw himself backwards and extracted the two guns from his waistband. As he fell, he aimed at each guard and fired simultaneously. Both centre mass. Both direct heart shots. Clean kills.

When he hit the ground, he didn't roll. With his back on the sand, Bishop aimed his pistols over his head at the upside down Red Beard, who was clawing for his side-arm. Bishop's move had given him time to react, but not enough to aim.

Bishop fired two shots into the centre of his chest. A fraction of a second too late, Red Beard fired wildly, then collapsed forward and slid down the dune, face down and motionless.

The excruciating pain in Bishop's thigh told him he'd been hit. He lifted his leg and the intense pain caused him to slam his fist into the sand. It was painful, but didn't appear to have hit bone. Probably. Then again, that could be the shock.

Gritting his teeth, Bishop righted himself and brushed off the sand. The wound was agonising but he had to keep moving. His pistols weren't silenced; others would arrive soon. He hobbled about, wincing as he assessed the bodies for any sign of life. There was none.

Standing over Red Beard, he finished his lesson. "Never take your eye off them."

In the dull moonlight, Bishop searched the ground for the pen he'd thrown into the air. Managing to find it, he shook it clean and slipped it into his pocket. It was the Mandarin Oriental pen Astrid had presented to him with such fanfare, seemingly a lifetime ago. She had been right. It really was mightier than a sword.

Limping up the hill, Bishop saw that he was only a short distance from the highway. Once over the next crest he'd call Zoya to come and pick him up. With any luck he would be clear in minutes, then he could pick up Oleg, get to the hotel, fix up his leg and down a bottle of scotch. But first, he had to survive the next few minutes. The noise he'd made and the injury inflicted lessened his chances significantly. Pushing through the agonising pain, he limped on.

An explosion in the distance reminded Bishop of the timer he'd set. He hoped it would be a further distraction.

On the crest of a dune, Bishop saw a figure stalking through the night. If the moon hadn't been behind the figure he never would have seen it; it moved so stealthily. It was the grey-hooded figure, the assassin who had taken out Demir, had likely kidnapped Astrid, and had killed Roll-Your-Own. The sniper was between Bishop and the road. The MI6 agent gripped his pistols tighter.

Game on, you bastard.

Losing sight of his target as he descended a dune, Bishop mentally calculated the various strategic positions where his foe could be. He was reasonably sure he hadn't been seen, but couldn't be certain, especially after the gunfight he'd had. All thoughts of the pain in his thigh were forgotten as he practically ran to his strategic location. He had to beat the bastard to the next dune, then he'd have the high ground. He could fire on the hooded figure before they knew what had hit them. This was it, his one chance.

Flopping on top of the dune, gun drawn, Bishop waited for the assassin to come over the crest. He realised he was overlooking the highway on his right. First he'd take his revenge, then he'd call Zoya. He was really going to enjoy that scotch. All he had to do was take the shot. Just one would do it. Aiming his pistol, he waited.

But no one came over the crest.

He was taking too long.

Where was the grey-hooded figure?

They should have come over the dune by now.

But if they hadn't... that meant...

Bishop turned as the butt of a rifle swung towards his head. His reaction was too slow. He only managed to duck part of the blow; the rifle butt glanced off his skull. The pistol was kicked from his hand.

Bishop launched himself at the hooded figure. They tumbled down the dune, plummeting towards the road.

As they fought and rolled, the world became flashes of moonlight and flying sand. Grunts and desperate blows were exchanged as they tumbled. When they reached the bottom of the dune, Bishop's head struck the road. The grey-hooded figure was on top. Bishop bucked them off and scrambled for the gun tucked down the back of his pants.

"Looking for this?"

That voice? It couldn't be...

Standing, the grey-hooded figure held Bishop's pistol. It was aimed at his head.

With their free hand, the figure pulled back the grey hood. The hammer on Bishop's pistol was pulled back.

"Time to die, lover." Astrid issued a sinister smile.

CHAPTER NINE

"Wait. Wait."

Bishop's brain was trying to catch up. The hooded figure, the one from the estate, the railway station, the dunes, was Astrid. She had never been stalked by a grey-hooded figure. It was her all along.

"Why didn't you kill me at the train station?"

Astrid crinkled her nose in amusement, an action Bishop had once found adorable. "Out of all the questions you could possibly ask, that's the one you go with?"

The gun in her hand hung motionless. There was no quiver; it wasn't heavy or unfamiliar in her hand.

"Just wondering. You seem awfully keen at the moment to put a bullet in me." Bishop's words were casual, but his eyes searched for a weapon, any weapon. "Yet at the station you could have taken me out, but you chose the gent we were about to interrogate."

Astrid rolled her eyes. "What can I say? I was momentarily overcome with sentimentality."

"And now?"

The gun barrel inched closer. "The moment has passed."

The face before Bishop was completely foreign. It had the exact same beautifully crafted features, but was bereft of all tenderness, humour and sympathy. It was a harsh, unforgiving face, one without mercy, without pity.

An occasional car or lorry sped down the highway, but none stopped. They were either oblivious to the forthcoming execution or indifferent. Lying on the ground injured and without weapons, Bishop saw no way out. Even his charm would not thaw Astrid's cold, wrathful stare.

With a bored sigh, as if keen to get it over with, Astrid asked, "Any last words?"

From the corner of his eye, Bishop saw a car with a single headlight.

"As a matter of fact, yes." Bishop propped himself up on an elbow and nodded. "Goodbye, Astrid."

Curiosity creased her face. Astrid tilted her head. "What's that supposed to—"

The car skidded sideways, slowing its momentum, but when it hit her, the glancing blow was enough to send her flying. Astrid careened 5 metres before thumping into the sand dune, where she lay motionless.

Staggering upright, Bishop saw the beaming face behind the wheel of the taxi. Wincing through the pain, Bishop limped over to the driver's side.

"You want a taxi, Mister?" Zoya's white teeth positively shone.

Bishop scowled. "I thought I told you to get far away from here."

Zoya shrugged. "Yeah, I'm terrible at following instructions. As my teacher at school always said, *look out!*"

For a fraction of a second Bishop wondered why Zoya's teacher had told her to look out. Then the windscreen exploded.

He dove for the ground. The gunshots echoed through the night air, there was no doubt where they had come from. Astrid stood unsteadily, holding the pistol with two hands. Her clothes were ripped and blood coated half her face from some unseen wound. She staggered forward, firing relentlessly into the taxi. Her eyes blazed with unhinged fury.

When the bullets stopped, Bishop rose shakily to his feet. He hesitantly examined the interior of the taxi. The driver was riddled with red bullet holes, her lifeless eyes staring at the distant stars.

Zoya was dead.

"The fucking bitch hit me with a car!" Astrid limped towards the taxi. She wiped her forehead, assessing the blood on her fingers, then turned to Bishop and completely transformed. In an instant her face was nearly the same lovely one Bishop remembered. "It really irritates me when people run me over."

In Bishop's expert opinion, she was deranged. Completely tonto. There was something else she was, too: out of bullets. Rage-shooting Zoya had spent the last of her ammunition.

Bishop was injured, but so was she. The playing field had been levelled. Plus, she had just killed his friend, and she'd nearly killed him, more than once. Normally Bishop found the idea of hitting a woman completely abhorrent. He was willing to forgo that just this once.

Standing to his full height, Bishop clenched his shaking fists, his anger barely contained. He had years of experience in controlling his emotions for the benefit of the Service, but he was ready to forget it all for revenge.

Instead of showing fear, Astrid smiled. A beaming, stunning smile. "You took your sweet time."

Too late, Bishop realised Astrid wasn't addressing him. Before he could turn, a sack was thrown over his head and he took several body blows that buckled his legs. Fighting both his sightlessness and the new assailant, Bishop struggled in what he knew was a losing battle. This new adversary was fresher and stronger, while the spy was close to spent.

In quick succession Bishop's hands and feet were bound and he was thrown into the back of some sort of van. As he struggled, gathering the fortitude to fight back, a needle pierced his upper arm, and the darkness grew darker still.

With Herculean effort, Bishop tried to pry his groggy eyes open. Thoughts muddied, he was unsure where he was or how long he'd been out. Did all those events even happen? Did he dream them? Was he in a hotel room? His own bed?

It took a while for his eyes to adjust to the gloom, and it was indeed gloomy. As gloomy as it got. He knew where he was.

He wished he didn't.

"Awake? Excellent. We may commence."

Once, Bishop had found the voice musical, angelic. Who was he kidding? It was still lovely. The difference was, now he knew it came from the fiery depths of hell.

Astrid limped forward, emerging from the shadows of Temple's dungeon. Apart from the limp, she seemed unharmed by her earlier altercation.

Bishop lay on the wooden torture table, his ankles and wrists manacled. His head throbbed from whatever drug they had given him, but that was nothing compared to the fire in his thigh. Nausea lurked around him, ready to pounce at any moment. He struggled against it. There were more important battles to fight.

Astrid traced her blood-red nails along Bishop's arm. "I'm going to go out on a limb and guess you're no stranger to being tied up?"

"Perhaps. But I usually like to take it in turns." Bishop's mouth was dry and metallic. "How about you go first? I'm a bit out of sorts."

Letting loose one of her full-throated laughs, Astrid shook her head humorously, as if Bishop had told a delightful witticism at a garden party. She had changed her clothes. She wore a pleasant sundress, in stark contrast to the surrounds. She'd cleaned herself up after Zoya's act of bravery.

Zoya.

Bishop's hands lunged for Astrid's flawless neck, but the chains jerked his hands to a halt before they could reach her. Knowing it was hopeless, he tried again, imagining Astrid's face as he squeezed the life from it. He fell back, exhausted by his futile efforts.

Tutting, Astrid glided around the table. Her delicate fingers slid over his body, along his arms, down his chest. Without hesitation, her fingers found the front of his trousers and traced circles over his groin. Bishop didn't need to think of cricket. Receiving no reaction, Astrid's hand slithered towards the bullet hole in his thigh. Without warning, she dug her thumb deep into the wound.

Bishop screamed like he never had before. Agonising. Primal. Astrid's eyes and mouth flew wide open, relishing the reaction. Her expression of ecstasy was close to the one he had seen on her face before, its source completely different. The elation on display now was nothing short of evil. Pure malevolence. There was no doubt: Astrid was a sadist.

He was right to have been wary on first meeting her. Her approaches had put him on guard, but he hadn't listened to his gut. He would remember that lesson for the rest of his life. He gave it two hours, tops.

The next few hours would be as painful as they would be final. No one knew where Bishop was. The only humans who knew of Temple's sadistic room were 3000 kilometres away. Even if they launched a rescue mission, it would come long after Astrid had played out her sick game. Oleg had traipsed off several kilometres in the opposite direction and knew nothing of the underground chamber, if he even thought of Temple's mansion at all. Despite knowing all this, Bishop wished Oleg would come bursting in, guns blazing. Bishop was willing to grasp to any glimmer of hope, even if it was graceless and Russian.

In the silence following his screams, Bishop heard shuffling behind him. The slow steady footfalls grew louder.

"Don't play too rough yet, my beloved, he has information we need."

Temple stepped forward, and his hand slithered around Astrid's waist. She turned and the two embraced passionately, their tongues intertwined, their breathing heavy. Bishop was reasonably sure they were about to do it right on the table on top of him.

Temple broke loose and stared at Bishop while Astrid straightened her clothes.

He checked his watch and addressed Astrid. "As fun as this will be, don't forget you have a plane to catch."

She pouted in reply, seeming disappointed to have to rush Bishop's torture. Try as he might, Bishop found it hard to feel sorry for her.

Temple turned to Bishop. "My beloved told me about your tussle on the dunes. I cannot believe you took out Peter Rob and his men but failed to take out my love here. And he's one tough son of a bitch. Quite remarkable, yes? It's almost as though you have feelings for her, a sentiment I can appreciate but can't condone. You understand, of course?"

"It wasn't our first tussle, though not as sweaty as the last." Bishop attempted to sound casual, as much as one could when shackled in a torture chamber awaiting death.

Temple's head snapped around and he glared at Astrid. In return, she demurely cast him an impish grin. It didn't seem to work. He huffed and it seemed to Bishop that Temple was unaware of Astrid's exploits. There was tension there. A fracture Bishop could exploit? Best-case scenario, they stab one another to death. And one of them throws Bishop the shackle key as their last dying act after making him a daiquiri of some description. Granted, it was unlikely, but it was a best-case scenario, after all.

With his mouth slanted to one side, Bishop gave a tsk. He spoke to Astrid. "You didn't tell him about our tryst? I can't imagine it was because you were embarrassed. That's not your style."

Astrid did her best to ignore him, concentrating instead on Temple's chest. Seductively, she ran her fingers down it, as if attempting to distract him from the revelation. It didn't work. Temple positively seethed.

Bishop addressed Temple. "So, she didn't tell you of our sweaty evening the night before last? Surprising. My god, I thought we were going to be tossed out of the hotel with all the hollering. She's quite the screamer when she's excited, isn't she?"

"That's enough," Astrid spat, then calmed herself. She slid her arm around Temple's shoulder and turned his head to kiss him slowly, tenderly.

Temple replied amiably, his tension eased but not abated. It seemed she had him on a leash.

She turned to Bishop. "Hate to tell you, lover, I faked every orgasm."

"No." Bishop glared at her. "You didn't. I'm experienced enough to know the difference."

Astrid laughed, but there was an edge to it, a tinge that betrayed the truth.

The MI6 agent scoured the two for reactions, anything he could use. "A new lover might fake for expediency or politeness, but there's no need. Soon, when she really experiences true bliss, I know her true unfiltered self in all its glorious unbridled honesty. There are some things you just can't fake."

Temple watched the exchange, wary. He still seethed at Astrid's actions, but chose to say nothing.

Forgoing a laugh, Astrid waved a dismissive hand. "You're quite charming."

"Thank you."

"I hadn't finished. You're quite charming," she smirked, but her eyes were devoid of humour, "but stupid. My team have facial recognition software running for all new entries into Marrakech. You popped up as a potential spy, as did Mikhail. That's why I spoke to you at the airport, no other reason."

And Oleg at the hotel, no doubt, Bishop thought. He noted she used his alias, so perhaps her intelligence wasn't as comprehensive as she thought.

"Once I took you to bed you couldn't wait to tell me you weren't an advertising executive. You may as well have handed over your ID card then and there. That's why I was suspicious of you to begin with, and that's why I slept with you. Your failing is your faith in your charm. You ate up the innocent dove routine like a hungry fat man at a wedding buffet."

"I don't think that's—"

"Stupid." Astrid cut him off, annoyed. "You had all

that time with me but considered me a naive schoolgirl caught up in events I was too innocent and foolish to appreciate. How very, very wrong of you. It seems there are things I *can* fake, Mr Charles Bishop of MI6." Despite his best efforts, Bishop must have reacted. Astrid seized upon it. "Oh yes, we know who you are now. We've had the suspicion confirmed and know far more than that tiny brain of yours could possibly comprehend."

There was no use asking where they'd obtained their information, they wouldn't divulge anything. But that didn't mean a man couldn't at least try to find out more.

Addressing Temple, Bishop asked, "What is it you want to achieve?"

"World domination."

"Really?"

"No," Temple chuckled, "but that's what you expected me to say, isn't it? A mad unscrupulous plan for world ascendency with some sort of warped ideology and whatnot? That's what you believed, right?"

In actuality, Bishop hadn't thought that far ahead, though it was obvious Temple believed he had. Bishop had spent all his efforts on trying to find out what the auction was; he'd assumed more would be discovered once he had that information. As it turned out, he was indeed right, only it was a bit more painful and fatal than he'd hoped. Which was a shame. Bishop always liked being right.

Temple and Astrid must believe Bishop knew more than he actually did, hence the upcoming interrogation and torture. It wasn't his dashing good looks and prowess in the bedroom that had spared his life until now, it was their need to extract information. They would want to know what Demir had told him, what MI6 knew, who else was after them. Even if he chose to tell them all he knew, it wouldn't be enough. They would assume there was more and torture him until his dying breath to get it out of him. Not that he was going to give them anything. Bishop was resigned to his fate, but that didn't mean he was going to make it easy for them.

Astrid ran her fingers along the inside of Bishop's leg. "It's a shame, though."

"What is?" Bishop thought Astrid seemed far too pleased with herself.

"I mean," Astrid stopped touching Bishop and ran her fingers down Temple's chest instead, "you and Oleg no longer being partners."

The manner in which she declared it put Bishop on edge. The confidence in the statement. The irrevocability of it.

She went on. "I have to say, when the two of you teamed up, the results were," she turned her sultry eyes to Bishop, "formidable. But it's all done with now, isn't it? Oleg put up a gallant fight, he was nothing if not tenacious."

Bishop's stomach fell. "Was?"

"Yes." She frowned girlishly and waggled her shoulders. "I'm afraid your bosom buddy didn't fare too well. He gave us one hell of a tussle though, I'll give him that. Took out a whole mess of our men before he was done." Her expression turned dark, practically gleeful. "But done it is. I'm afraid there won't be a white knight swinging in on a vine to save you. You are utterly alone."

Bishop shook his head. "It doesn't make sense."

"There aren't many places to hide in the desert. We tracked him down and—"

"No, not that. The white knight swinging on a vine thing. That's mixing your metaphors to an appalling degree. Have a white night saving, sure, but the Tarzan illusion with the vine makes it a lazy metaphor, not to mention contradictory. Imagine the extra weight of the suit of armour? And let's not even get into the subject of jock sweat. It's very confusing, is all I'm saying."

If Astrid had meant to alarm him by mentioning Oleg's passing, Bishop was determined not to show it. He'd given her far too much already. Below his bravado, Bishop was indeed alarmed. There had been the tiniest glimmer of hope that Oleg would come to his rescue if he somehow made his way to the villa without transport, and also miraculously discovered the torture room. Now even that implausible prospect was dashed.

Bishop was alone. He would die alone. Just like he always knew he would.

As for Oleg's passing, Bishop didn't know how to feel about it. He almost certainly despised the Russian. Never trusted him. It was because of him that the whole mission had been blown. And yet, Bishop still felt remorse at his death. If he had more time, perhaps he could explore that. He didn't, so he moved on.

"Why fake your own kidnapping?"

Astrid rolled her eyes as if the question was simplistic. "It kept you occupied, didn't it? Had you running around solving that particular puzzle while ignoring others."

She had a point. They had wasted too much time searching for her. When they stumbled on the thugs at the station who could have provided answers, she shut them down without mercy.

Still wishing to delay the inevitable for as long as possible, Bishop decided to change the subject. "So, what was really going on in the tent? You weren't auctioning salt and pepper shakers, we all know you were selling commodities far more valuable."

Bishop didn't want to reveal that he had no idea what those commodities were. They clearly assumed Bishop knew more, so he would play into it. If they thought MI6 was better informed than they were, they might be forced into acting rashly.

A flash of red smacked across Astrid's face. "You are not the interrogator here!" Her lungs heaved, her features flushed. "What the fuck is it with *your* questions? *You* are the one tied up. *You* are the one being given the third degree, not the other way around!"

She had a temper. Bishop would remember that. Perhaps he could use it. Even now, in the precarious position he was in, he strategized.

Ignoring the tirade, he kept his tone civil, as if Astrid's outburst hadn't occurred at all. He turned to Temple. "You really think with all those people attending the auction it was going to remain secret? Ministers of defence, of finance. You've grown too big, drawn too much attention. You are out of the shadows whether you like it or not. There's no scurrying back now. Your time is done and you know it."

He highly doubted they did, but Bishop thought he may as well try to convince them. Better to fill them with dread, and hope they made a mistake that would be their undoing.

Temple waved a dismissive hand, his features patronising, like he was addressing a child. "Nothing you saw was illegal. A simple auction of antiques for anyone watching. Even if someone could connect the dots to its real purpose, they would be hard pressed to prove it. Our tracks are too well covered. Our organisation, our people are perfect."

Bishop shook his head. "There are certain things that are perfect. A cup of Earl Grey on a winter's morning. James Brown's horn section. This lady's arse." Astrid smiled but said nothing. He went on. "But people are most certainly not perfect. They make mistakes, their values and priorities shift, or they see the writing on the wall and do what they must to protect themselves. Your little empire is not as perfect as you think it is."

The two exchanged glances. That had them thinking. Just like Oleg's subtle mention of a mole at MI6, the mere thought had planted a seed. Bishop intended on watering it. Had someone in their organisation been compromised? If so, who? What had they told? Their imaginations would be running wild.

"Despite your precautions we know perfectly well what you were auctioning. You may as well have held it at Scotland Yard. Your overpriced little sale wasn't as secret as you think."

"Overpriced?" Temple snorted. "Really? I thought he got the plans to the Black Falcon at a bargain basement price. Our fault for placing it at the start of the auction, I guess. Live and learn."

Astrid nudged him and issued a frown. Project Black Falcon was the US Air Force's next generation top-secret war plane, the latest stealth fighter. If Kali had their hands on the plans, that was a monumental coup. Not even Congress knew what the plane looked like or had seen any specs. Whoever could replicate the plans would have the biggest military leg-up of the century. Temple was right, a hundred million was a bargain.

He's talking, good. Use that.

"I had all the other items, but I missed what the second was."

"The defence system upgrade specially designed to detect and destroy the Falcon fighters."

"Why are you telling him this?" Astrid pursed her lips.

Amusement creasing his features, Temple replied, "Because I get to say the best part." He turned to Bishop. "It doesn't work. Not as far as we've been able to determine, anyway. The price kept going up. It was all I could do to keep a straight face. Amazing."

What Bishop would have given to be able to punch the smug grin off the arms dealer's face. The arrogance was sickening. He did his best to stay on topic.

"Whether it works or not, why would the Pakistani government need it?" Bishop thought for a moment. "Wait, not the government, a Defence Minister with a coup d'état on his mind. Okay, that makes more sense. What better way to bolster support for your military junta than by taking down the US's shiny new technological wonder? Maybe it wasn't so wild. I wonder who's funding his little buying spree?"

"It is not my place to ask questions. I am but a humble merchant."

"You're dying for me to say merchant of death, aren't you?"

"I am supplying select members of the international community with what they need. At a fair market price, of course."

"A fair market price?"

"Simple capitalism, isn't it? The Pakistani representative wanted firepower superiority. He bought the chance to give a superpower a bloody nose. He bought power."

"He bought a dud. And a doll."

"And a doll, yes." Temple gave Bishop an arrogant look, like an adult humouring a child who had failed to land a joke. "Very good. She said you were funny. I thought she was being magnanimous."

This went way beyond arms dealing. Selling the ability to take on a superpower went further than supplying a few crates of surplus rocket launchers. This was world shaping. Temple had joked about world domination, but this wasn't far off. The fact that other traders had retired or gone missing meant this was a power play, no matter how he chose to downplay it. Kali meant to reshape the world from the shadows.

Bishop was reminded of what Demir had disclosed before his untimely death. "A humble merchant won't deliberately sell to your enemy twice as much if you fail to meet their excessive terms."

Temple frowned. "There are no rules to say who an arms dealer can trade with."

"Yes there are. Hundreds of them. The US Gun Control Act, for one, and that's for licenced dealers." Bishop shook his head. "Kali aren't known or licenced. The former has already happened, which means the latter will never occur. Your clock is ticking, you just don't know it."

"I'm not worried about the US government." Temple's face showed no hint of sarcasm.

"Not worried about…" Bishop was unconvinced. "They have a few resources, they might come knocking. Say hi for me."

Believing Temple would be disinclined to expand further, Bishop dropped the subject. Aware his own time was coming to an end, and that the torture would start at any moment, Bishop had one last question. "The third lot, the delivery to the Saudis. We all know it was more than a mere lamp." Bishop distinctly remembered the words "arrange delivery within a week" being uttered by Temple during the auction.

Astrid stepped forward and crossed her arms. "What was in the third lot, Bishop?"

"Oh, you know as well as I do."

It was if the room had grown several degrees cooler. He felt an uncharacteristic need to tug his collar.

Astrid's gaze was unflinching. After several uncomfortable seconds, a slow grin creased her beautiful features. "You don't know a thing, do you?" The amused expression enveloped her face and she crinkled her nose. "Oh, you silly, silly man. Were you honestly trying to interrogate us? How precious. You're like a lab rat who thinks he can outsmart the scientist. You must know, no matter what you do you're going to be sliced up by the end of this. Surely you know that? I'm bored playing nice and offering you cheese, little ratty." Astrid extracted the biggest blade from the table of torture. "Time for your tests to really begin."

She turned to Temple. "What's the time?"

He checked his watch. "Ten past five."

Bishop had been out for a while, no wonder he was groggy.

"Damn." She glanced between the knife and Bishop. "We've played nice too long. We have to get a shift on. Can you check my flight is still on time? I'd hate to rush my enjoyment if I don't have to."

Without a word, Temple bowed and left. With the two of them alone, the torture chamber suddenly seemed even frostier. Astrid turned slowly towards Bishop, a wry smile on her red lips. She strode towards him, her hips swinging confidently.

In a voice that was almost a purr, she asked, "You really think I have a perfect arse?"

"I can say without a word of a lie it is a thing of beauty. I don't like to brag, but I'm somewhat of an authority on the subject."

Astrid giggled. For the briefest of moments, Bishop thought of her as the perfect creature he had first met. Too much had changed since then, but for a fraction of a second he relished the illusion.

There was one more thing for Bishop to try. It was a Hail Mary combined with a last-minute pass at the eleventh hour with more than a dash of desperation. He had no more cards to play. He was about to bluff with a two. Not even a pair of twos.

He spoke in his most seductive tone. "You didn't shoot me at the railway. You didn't shoot me at the dunes, either. You had chances but didn't take them. I have to wonder why."

Astrid tilted her head, amused. "Oh god, is this where you ask if I love you or something? Please don't, I'm nauseous enough already. Someone hit me with a car earlier and I'm not quite myself."

In spite of her smile, the coldness remained. The woman had utterly fooled him. That had never occurred before. In other circumstances he would be impressed. The woman was indeed unique.

"What's the deal with Temple? You work for him and he checks your flights?"

Astrid's face was creased in confusion. "Work for…?"

"The head of Kali seems more of an accountant than I would have thought."

The giggle returned, this time unhindered by humour. "I don't work for Temple." Without warning Astrid leapt onto the table and straddled Bishop, the soft skin of her thighs resting on his hips. "He's not the head of Kali, you silly man. I thought you were talking to him too much." She tilted her head curiously. "You don't know a thing, do you? What, you thought because he's the man he must be in charge, is that it? How very tiny minded of you."

As Astrid stared down at Bishop the light illuminated the back of her head. She played with the knife in her hands, the blade gleaming. The knife edge came to his neck. Bishop dared not move a muscle.

Slowly, precisely, Astrid drew the blade across his neck, shaving him in a dangerously slow movement. Her eyes told him she relished the sight of the blade against his skin. It nicked his throat and Bishop flinched. She lifted the knife, and with a fascinated expression examined his blood as it ran down the steel.

Head turned, she finally looked him in the eye. "No, my love." She licked the blood off the blade. "I am Kali."

Without waiting for a reaction she plunged the blade into his side. Bishop screamed like he never had in his life. Astrid's eyes blazed with ecstasy.

CHAPTER TEN

Time was an illusion. Its passing meant nothing to Bishop. All he knew was pain. Mind-numbing, excruciating pain.

Bishop had no idea how long he had endured the brutal torture, the agonising incisions to his body. He was sure somewhere in the world someone would be aware of the passage of time. Bishop would never meet them. Not that he wanted to. All he wished for was death.

If anyone was to ask, he would embrace death like an old lover. He would dive headlong into the abyss without hesitation.

But no one asked.

He had progressed far beyond the point of endurance. If he were capable, he would beg for it to end, but he was beyond even that.

Bishop shouldn't have lasted this long. No human being should have. He wasn't thankful for his body's endurance, he cursed it.

All was still. He had been left alone with his agony. Astrid and Temple had taken turns torturing him. It was beyond pleasure for them. The gratification each took from his agonised screams only multiplied his dread, his acceptance of the inevitable.

His initial bravado had long since been stripped away. When he first talked to them, they had been playing with him. They let him talk. They responded, giving him hope that he could find a way out. But it was all deception. There was only one way out.

Bishop's left eye must have been bloodshot, everything was tinged red and opaque. The gunshot wound in his leg was open and weeping. The knife gash in his side felt like it was on fire.

His questions had stopped when he could no longer form words, only guttural, primal noises. That hadn't halted his torment, though; it had only multiplied it. They wanted to see how far they could push him, how long he could endure. He was their plaything. A screaming, writhing plaything.

The distant sound of a creaking door poked his drowsy senses. The sound of footsteps heightened it. It was ridiculous. He still held out hope that Paul or a fellow MI6 agent or an entire unit of Royal Marine Commandos would crash through the door at any moment. At this stage he'd settle for a Teletubbie with a butter knife.

As the footfalls grew louder he could see that the person's frame was large. *Temple.* Before the gruesome twosome had left together, Bishop vaguely recalled a comment about a plane flight. Astrid must have been packing. He hoped she dressed warm, he'd hate for her to catch a cold.

Temple must have been there to finish him off. Then again, that may have been the optimism talking. Optimism was a curse. Bishop had no reserves left to call on. He was done.

The figure approaching was a blur. Bishop couldn't even make out if he had a cloak and a scythe.

The shadow sighed. "You are hideous."

It wasn't a French accent. It may have been the delirium, but Bishop could have sworn...

"Were you put in a blender? It looks like you were placed in a blender."

With a level of concentration Bishop thought he no longer possessed, he focused on the face before him. It grimaced. It was an austere, polite grimace. The big Russian set to work on the manacles securing Bishop to the table.

Through the haze of pain, Bishop managed to wheeze out, "Thank you."

"You saved my life, so I owed you." Oleg shrugged as he unclipped the shackles. "We are even. Do not expect this to happen again."

Bishop rubbed his unchained wrists. "They said you were dead."

"They?"

"Temple and Astrid. They are Kali."

Oleg stopped unhooking Bishop's ankles. "Astrid is the enemy?"

Bishop nodded. "She's Kuolema, the head of Kali." He sat up. The movement made him light-headed. He fought the nausea attacking his senses, attempted to gain focus, to stay alert.

"They may have said I'm dead, but I am not." Oleg freed Bishop's last limb and winked. "Although I thought I may have been for some time. I was hunted. When I headed south I found tyre tracks to mask my prints. Their resources were spread thin and they must have missed me. I was fortunate, I think. When our taxi did not arrive, I hitchhiked back here."

"Zoya is dead. Astrid killed her."

"She killed the child? Is she truly that evil?"

For a second, Bishop relived every knife thrust and maniacal laugh he had endured over the last few hours. "You have no idea."

Inhaling deeply, Bishop sat up, agony ripping through him. It felt as if red-hot pokers were being plunged into every incision in his body. Steadying himself, the pain ebbed and he regained a semblance of composure.

Bishop coughed. He brought up bile and blood. "How did you know where to find me?"

"There weren't many places you could have been. Temple left in his car a while ago; he had a companion I did not see. It must have been Astrid. I waited to ensure there was no one else, then came searching for you down here."

"Wait… how did you even know there was a dungeon at all?"

Oleg's mouth twisted sideways into a sheepish smirk.

"Did you hack our systems? Was it the mole?" At that stage, Bishop wouldn't have cared if it was.

"No, nothing so elaborate. I placed security cameras in your hotel room to observe your security devices."

"When did you… your hand. That's how you injured your hand, breaking into my hotel room?"

Oleg shrugged. "Da."

"You sneaky son-of-a-bitch."

"I am a spy."

"That's what I said."

Gingerly, Oleg helped Bishop swing his legs over the side of the table. "Can you stand?"

Bishop raised an eyebrow. "If it means getting out of here, I can fly."

"Walking will be sufficient."

Wincing, Bishop shuffled forward to place his feet on

the ground and let out a cry of pain, so overcome he didn't care that Oleg had seen his weakness. He was far beyond caring.

Somehow managing to stand, he put an arm around the big man and leaned on him to remain upright. The two shuffled a few steps, Bishop sucking in deep breaths through his teeth with every stride. He could do this.

"What the hell?"

The two spies spun around. Temple stood in the doorway, knife in hand. Oleg let go of Bishop. With nothing to hold onto, Bishop fell, grasping the air for support that didn't come. He landed hard on the ground.

Oleg yanked his pistol from his shoulder holster and fired. Temple's head jerked back and his body collapsed, just like Bishop's had. But unlike Bishop, he would never rise again. The bullet to the centre of his forehead had seen to that.

Gun trained on his target, Oleg approached slowly, ensuring the kill with another three bullets. There was no need to check for a pulse.

"Not so good at preserving witnesses, are you?"

Oleg turned. "You would prefer I hit him with a pillow, perhaps?"

"He was our only witness."

"There is also Astrid, da?"

"True. But we have to find her first."

"When I observed Temple, he placed luggage in the rear of his vehicle."

"We need to get to the airport."

Oleg frowned. "We need to get you to the hospital."

"Stitches can wait. Revenge can't."

But revenge didn't come. At least, not yet. Despite racing to the airport, there was no trace of Astrid. Her flight must have left before they arrived. She had mentioned she was cutting it fine to get to the airport. Only two international flights had recently departed: New York and Abu Dhabi.

On the way to the airport, Bishop had bandaged himself as Oleg drove. He needed stitches and urgent medical attention, but patching would postpone it for a time. He'd cleaned himself up as best he could, but knew he was unfit to be seen. Fit to be shunned, sure, but not seen.

After failing to find her at the airport, Oleg drove away, the mood in the car sombre. Using Oleg's phone, he called MI6 and was put through to Paul. Before his boss said a word, Bishop advised him that the line was not secure, much to the Russian's amusement. Providing a succinct summary, he gave Paul a rundown of recent events.

Paul promised to have agents waiting for both flights. At Bishop's urging, he assured him they would take every precaution, given Astrid's true nature.

"You didn't listen," Paul said over the phone.

"Listen to what?"

"That message I sent you, when you first arrived. I distinctly remember wishing you good luck and advising you not to get shot."

"I was never very good at following instructions."

Paul let the silence swirl for a moment. "We'll get her, Bishop."

Before he hung up, Bishop told Paul about the recorded footage from the auction and urged MI6 to open a new avenue of investigation. Paul assured his agent he would get right on it. The two rang off.

Feeling suddenly dizzy, Bishop leaned against the car window. With no other options, he relented to Oleg's demands and went to hospital.

There he was prodded and poked and injected. Not unfamiliar sensations, although at least he had the benefit of painkillers this time. One doctor repeatedly asked a nurse how Bishop wasn't dead already. Not exactly an ideal bedside manner.

Hours ticked by, and eventually word came through. Astrid had not deplaned at New York or Abu Dhabi. The head of Kali was a ghost.

Bishop had to mend his body. Over the next few hours he let the doctors do what they needed to heal him. Oleg left and Bishop was alone in a hospital room for the second time in a week. On both occasions Astrid had put him there.

Never again would he underestimate the purveyor of his current pain. He closed his eyes to get some rest. Bishop would need all his strength hunt her down.

Bishop awoke to the sounds of screams. It took several moments to realise they were his own, and much longer to calm his frayed nerves. He had to convince himself he was no longer on the torture table. While this was true, the after-effects were still very much present.

His pain had eased, but not his dread. There was nothing broken, the stitches were mending well. Having been pumped full of antibiotics and saline, he was infection free and on the road to recovery. At least, his body was.

On the bedside table a small jar glistened in the morning sunlight. It contained the fragments of the bullet taken from his thigh—a souvenir of his time in Marrakech. He would have been happy with a fridge magnet.

Mid-morning he had his first and only visitor. He came in and threw a bottle on the bed while Bishop finished the last of his bland hospital lunch.

"What, no flowers?" Bishop smirked.

Oleg shook his head. "Vodka is better." He slumped into the lone armchair.

"For once I'm not going to argue with you."

Bishop opened Oleg's present and took a swig straight from the bottle, then handed it over. Oleg did the same. They sat quietly for several minutes.

He still didn't trust the Russian. He had, after all, spied on him. Then again, he also saved his life when he really didn't need to. Oleg claimed it had been repayment of a debt, but was there more to it than that? Where they becoming friends? Bishop didn't know how to feel about that. He didn't want a new friend. He wanted something else.

"My organisation cannot find her." The Russian's words were morose.

It was as if Oleg had read Bishop's mind. "Mine either."

They passed the bottle between them and drank. It was unlikely Astrid would return to Temple's villa. If he didn't reply to her messaging, she would assume the worst and stay away. With her lover dead, there was no need to come back. That meant she could be anywhere on the planet.

Letting his mind wander, the MI6 agent went through all he knew. It wasn't a lot. There were fragments. More precisely, fragments of fragments. He sifted through them in his mind.

"There's a shipment," Bishop said.

"A shipment of what?"

"No idea." Bishop rubbed his eyes. "But during the auction the third lot had to be delivered within a week. That's what the lamp bought."

"I don't understand. How does this help—"

"The shipment was from this auction, so it can't be legitimate. Therefore, it's potentially something we could intercept. If we can do that, there's a chance, a small one I'll grant you, that the shipment could be traced back to its source. If we could do that, we could build a case against Kali and bring them down."

Bishop didn't need to add that it could lead them directly to Astrid herself.

"But what is the shipment?"

Bishop beamed. The expression must have been startling, because the Russian recoiled. "I don't know."

Oleg narrowed his gaze, amused. "Where is it?"

"I don't know that either." Bishop pushed the food tray away and ripped the biometric sensor pads off his chest. The room filled with various beeps and warning chimes. He ignored them and reached for his clothes.

In minutes he was dressed and vaguely presentable. Before leaving the room, he made sure he snatched the tiny vial with the bullet fragments. Fuel for his vengeance.

Over the howls of protest from doctors and nurses, Bishop left the hospital. Holding Oleg's shoulder for stability, the two hobbled towards the taxi stand outside the Polyclinic du Sud hospital.

The warm air refreshed him. It was good to be free of the confines of the sterile environment. He wasn't healed, far from it, but for the sake of his wellbeing, Bishop had to move. He needed to act. Bishop waved down a taxi. His road to recovery began here.

While they waited, Oleg grunted. "Where are we going, Englishman?"

Bishop grinned. "Do you want to go and kidnap the Saudi Finance Minister?"

Oleg's smile matched Bishop's. "More than anything in the world."

CHAPTER ELEVEN

To say the Royal Mansour Marrakech was opulent was an understatement in the extreme. It would be like stating that a DB9 was a mere car, or calling the Balvenie fifty-year-old single malt an adequate dram.

The Royal Mansour had been commissioned by King Mohammed VI himself, and he'd spared no expense. Set among 4 hectares of fragrant Moorish gardens, the hotel was an architectural masterpiece, adorned with amazing geometric mosaics, carved cedarwood, stained glass, beaten bronze and inlaid marquetry. Inside, the rooms were finely decorated with suede and silk carpets, velvet sofas and crystal chandeliers. It seemed fitting that the Saudi Finance Minister was staying at one of the most expensive hotels on the continent.

Inside, privacy was at an absolute premium. The elite guests the hotel attracted did not want to be confronted by the great unwashed, so the hotel had a network of subterranean passages for the staff to get about, so as to not offend the delicate sensibilities of the sickeningly rich. It was this last aspect that Bishop and Oleg planned to exploit.

The silver Airbus H155 that sat on the helipad told the two spies that the minister was yet to depart. That was unfortunate for him. Given his status and who he represented, security would be formidable, though not as determined as his brand-new adversaries.

In the second-storey bar across the street, Bishop and Oleg drank overpriced cocktails and waited. It was late, the air cool under the blanket of stars. The revelry of the bar had steadily waned and they were the last two customers left. Anxious staff hovered, waiting for the Westerners to finish their drinks so they could go home.

Bishop swirled the ice in his glass with a straw. "No killing hotel staff."

Oleg frowned. "If I have to—"

"No." Bishop stopped stirring and glared at the Russian. "They're just doing a job. They probably get paid fuck all to wait on arrogant pricks who demand room-temperature ice and shiatsu massages for their ocelots. They don't deserve a bullet in the back of the head for earning an honest wage."

Oleg shrugged. "Fine. No killing hotel staff."

"And the minister's entourage, if you can help it."

Oleg's mouth dropped open. "What if a fly buzzes past, can I swat it or will Your Zen Majesty object to the cosmic imbalance?"

Bishop snorted. "They work for a prick, that doesn't automatically mean they are one, okay? If there's no alternative, fine, but working for an arsehole doesn't mean they're the manifestation of evil."

The Russian groaned. "This is not an MI6 operation. You understand this, da?"

"Just tread carefully is all I'm saying, and try not to put a bullet in the face of the subject before we interrogate him. This is our last shot."

"I am aware of this." Oleg swirled his glass. He didn't

make eye contact. "Is this mission sanctioned by your government?"

"Officially or unofficially?"

"Either."

"No." Bishop was conscious of the time. "Are we doing this or not? I'll go alone if I have to."

"Have you seen your face? You resemble a child's piñata after all the candy fell out."

"Are you in?"

"I am, but only if I can call you Mr Piñata Face from now on."

Bishop ignored the jibe. The two finished their drinks and left a hefty tip. Making their way towards the high, ornately decorated fence of the hotel, Bishop felt oddly fresh. It may have been the booze, or the painkillers or adrenaline, but he didn't feel the full weight of his recent ordeal. The doctors had done a great job patching him up, but he had no time for rest and recuperation. That would happen one day, just not today.

Both he and Oleg wore black, and there the similarities ended. Again, Bishop was dressed in a manner befitting the luxuriant surrounds of the hotel: expensive slacks and shoes, a slim-cut long-sleeved black shirt. His counterpart, on the other hand, was dressed to clean the toilets of the same establishment. Black jeans, black runners and a t-shirt so stained Bishop first thought it was a Jackson Pollock homage.

They strolled through the front entrance like they owned the place. The cobblestone path was delicately lit and surrounded by lush palms and vegetation. It had a heady perfume of gardenias, and dripped with affluence. The spies held their heads high while checking for threats. Thankfully, none were immediately apparent.

On their first sighting of a "Staff Only" sign they split off from the path and ducked through the foliage. A far less attractive path was harshly lit. They followed it towards the main building. Far above them, the main entrance glowed with a soft, warm light. Below, the staff were made to scurry about in harsh fluorescent lighting interspersed with long patches of darkness. The Morlocks to the super-rich Eloi.

Near the subterranean entrance a young kid, about seventeen or so, stood smoking in the dark. Approaching slowly so as not to startle him, Bishop put on a friendly face.

On seeing him, the kid jumped, threw the cigarette on the ground and stubbed it out, his face pained. "You're not going to tell, are you? It's just the guests can, so I thought if it was near the balcony... I don't want to get fired... please don't say anything."

Bishop winked. "I won't if you don't."

Confusion creased the kid's face. "I don't want to get into trouble."

"No, of course not." Bishop's voice was calming, sympathetic. "And trouble is what we're trying to avoid as well, okay?" Bishop nodded his head towards Oleg as he stepped out of the shadows. "You know this man, of course?"

"I think... I think so?" The kid didn't want to offend by saying he didn't.

"He's a very big Hollywood producer, I knew you recognised him straight away. I'll be honest, he's in a spot of bother, you see. We're scouting locations with a past leading lady and he's late because he and the lady, who let's just say isn't his wife, have spent the afternoon... You don't need to know the details, but let's just say he shouldn't be seen coming in so late, okay? I'm sure you know there have already been too many scandals. One more and the studio—the one he founded, mind you—are going to fire his arse. My friend and I are keen to prevent that from happening, you see."

The kid nodded slowly. He got the gist, but that didn't mean he fully understood what it was they wanted.

"What movie are you making?"

"Uh, good question." Bishop rubbed the back of his neck. "I'm, uh, they're remaking *The Cannonball Run* with an all-star cast. Filming the whole thing in Africa—you know, subsidies and tax breaks and whatnot. Chris Pratt is in talks for the Burt Reynolds part, he's teaming up with Donald Glover. Emma Stone and Jennifer Lawrence in another car. You get the idea."

Oleg perked up. "I would watch that movie."

Bishop blinked at him. "I should hope so." He squinted. "As you're the one making it."

"Ha, yes, of course." Oleg straightened his back and turned to the kid. "I'm kind of a big deal."

Bishop stuffed a wad of notes in the young man's hand, sickened by the realisation that he had done the exact same thing to Zoya and now she was dead.

Patting the notes, Bishop said, "That's for helping us. Is it sufficient?"

Eyes wide, the kid stared at the cash and nodded.

"What's your name?"

"My name is Gabe, sir. I can get you what you need." A hopeful expression crossed his features. "When you make the movie, can I have a part? It doesn't even have to be a big one. I'll stand up the back, I don't have to say anything. My brother Jaheem would be so jealous!"

The kid's voice rose for the last part. Bishop nodded while shushing him. "Sure, absolutely. You have my solemn vow that if this particular movie ever gets made you get a speaking part."

This seemed to please him no end. The kid squinted at Bishop and his demeanour turned serious. "What happened to your…" He waved his hand around his own face.

"I also do stunt work on the side." Bishop leaned in close. "My advice to you is never work with Ryan Gosling, okay?"

Gabe nodded. "What do you need?"

Bishop slapped his hand down on his shoulder. "Two uniforms, a clipboard and a mop." He glanced down at the kid's hand. "Oh, and can I borrow your lighter?"

Gabe was true to his word, and in no time the two spies were dressed in crisp white uniforms, although the Russian's was somewhat snug. They navigated the subterranean labyrinth beneath the hotel with ease, thanks to Gabe. Other staff paid them no heed, too busy attending to the needs of the one per cent.

If he had to guess, Bishop would have said the Finance Minister had the Presidential Suite. He was awarded the grand total of nothing for being correct. Gabe had heard from other staff that the minister had a temper. He'd apparently flown into a rage when a cleaner had dared to leave behind a dusting cloth, and demanded her dismissal. The hotel had complied and she'd been fired on the spot. Apparently the whole hotel was on edge.

It was fortunate, as far as their mini-operation was concerned. Nobody particularly liked the minister and staff were only too happy to avoid that end of the hotel. Gabe led them from the underground passageway to near the suite. There they parted ways. Gabe had no desire to be near the wrathful guest, and Bishop wanted him nowhere near what they were about to do. They parted on a silent handshake, Gabe opening the hidden door to the opulent hallway.

The two spies strode down the luxuriously appointed hall near the minister's suite.

"You would have made a good socialist, I think."

Bishop glanced towards his companion. "I… what?"

Oleg shrugged. "You have no time for the bourgeois. The contempt you have for the rich. You always seem to side with the proletariat. This is odd for a capitalist swine, I think."

"Who are you kidding?" Bishop chuckled. "You're not from the USSR, don't tell me you represent the great Soviet State. You buy blue jeans like the rest of us."

"True, true. But you do not like the wealthy. So I am thinking it has to do with your past, why you do not like them? Hmmmm? Did a rich man steal your lollipop, Englishman?"

With a dismissive wave of his hand, Bishop rejected the notion. "I appreciate expensive things."

"Oh yes, just not the people who buy them."

Approaching the door, Bishop chose to focus on the matter at hand. Bursting in all guns blazing could easily start something; at the very least, an international incident, at worst, a war. Neither of those things would be welcome in his account of the mission, not that Bishop planned on including the next hour or so in his official MI6 report.

Two thick-necked guards stood on either side of the huge double doors. The spies didn't slow, theirs was purely a reconnaissance walk-by to get the lay of the land. The two guards were heavily armed. Submachine guns, sidearms, nightsticks. All designed for close quarters fighting. They were well trained, too. One kept an eye on them as they walked past, the other scanned for other threats. They were disciplined.

According to their sources, at least two more guards were inside the rooms, and there were two more roaming the halls at all times. A frontal assault would be costly and ill-advised. Bishop had been shot enough already on this mission.

From inside the room, there was a crash. Neither Bishop nor Oleg reacted. One of the guards flinched slightly, but remained stoic behind his aviator glasses.

Inside the room a loud voice shouted, "How hard can it be? Red! I said red. Not fucking whatever this is!"

Shuffling, followed by another crash. One of the huge doors swung open and a voluptuous auburn-haired beauty staggered out at speed, as if thrown. She wore an elegant sequinned gown that hugged her curves. One stiletto on her left foot, she clutched the other to her chest, along with her purse. Unsteady on her feet, she struggled to stand to put her other shoe on. Neither of the guards moved to assist her.

"Here." Bishop offered his arm.

The stunning woman smiled, though her eyes were pained. "Thank you, I…"

"No need. Let us escort you." Bishop eyed the guards. "Rough neighbourhood."

The woman slipped on her shoe and the three walked down the hall in silence.

Once out of earshot of the guards, Bishop asked, "Are you alright? Did he hurt you?"

Now fully composed, the woman replied, "No, I'm fine."

"The graze on your cheek says otherwise."

Her hand darted to her cheek. She pulled out a compact and checked it in the mirror, then tutted. Turning to Bishop, she nodded. "It looks like you've been knocked about a bit yourself."

"Let's say we've both had run-ins with undesirable

sorts of late." Bishop laid his hand over hers. "Did he touch you? In other ways?"

"No, it didn't get that far." She smiled broadly, a crinkle in the centre of her forehead, seemingly pleased by Bishop's concern. "Not his type apparently."

"Then the man is obviously a fool."

"My employer hoped he wouldn't notice; they were wrong." Her smile genuine now, she considered Bishop. "You're a smooth one. Thank you for your assistance. It seems my night wasn't totally wasted."

Oleg rolled his eyes and groaned.

"I don't believe any time with you would be wasted." Bishop noted that the woman hadn't relinquished hold of his arm.

Oleg leaned over to Bishop and murmured, "What are you doing?"

"Improvising."

Oleg frowned. "Is that what they call it in England?"

Originally the plan had been to impersonate hotel staff and infiltrate the minister's room. The clipboard was meant to signify Bishop's instructor status. The lighter was if that didn't work; when in doubt, burn the place down. Now the MI6 agent was formulating another plan.

The woman rubbed Bishop's arm. "Perhaps you could buy me a drink?"

"I must say I'm flattered, but paying is something I usually avoid, my good lady. But I am thankful for the offer."

"I only meant the drink; everything else is on the house. A girl can have fun in her own time, you know."

Issuing another grunt, Oleg muttered, "I wonder where they keep the sick bags."

Choosing to ignore the enticing invitation, as they walked down the corridor Bishop took note of which rooms had their "Do Not Disturb" signs illuminated and which had lights on. When they reached the end of the hall, Oleg pressed the button for the lift. He cast a glance back towards the minister's room.

"Getting through that door will be a problem. If we have a big enough surprise, we should be able to—"

"We're not going through the front door." Bishop wasn't facing Oleg, but the woman on his arm. She regarded him curiously, as if wondering why he was speaking to her.

"No?" Oleg's face creased into confusion.

"No." Bishop winked at the woman. "We're going to make him come to us."

"We are? And how do you plan on pulling off that miraculous feat?"

"Because we're going to give him exactly what he wants."

The room was softly lit. Red velvet walls and luxurious furnishings surrounded the central feature: an enormous four poster bed. Solid oak, intricately carved and draped in opaque silk chiffon, it dominated the room. The sweet smell of jasmine permeated the tranquil scene. The lighting was so dim it gave everything an ethereal feel.

The door clicked open and a sliver of light from the hallway invaded the tranquil scene. Tentatively, hesitantly, the interloper stalked into the room.

"Hello?" He closed the door behind him. "My name is Essam."

On the bed, a figure writhed under the covers. Essam grinned broadly and strode forward. He wore only a hotel robe and an eager expression. On the bed, the covers seductively folded open. An invitation.

"I do hope you're…" Essam peeked through the

canopy. "You *are* a redhead." His grin doubled. "I like redheads."

In the darkness of the room, Essam hefted himself onto the end of the massive bed and began crawling along it. "I do hope you've packed a toothbrush. You and I are going to be here a long time, little girl."

His prey writhed on the bed, flicking red curls seductively. Essam licked his lips. He stopped to untie his robe, exposing his pot belly. Waggling his eyebrows as if to say, *there's more where this came from*, he continued his approach.

With a growl, he leaned over the figure. "I've brought you a present." He slid his sweaty hand up and down the lapel of his gown. "Do you want to see my surprise?"

The redhead replied in a deep Russian accent, "I assure you, my surprise is bigger."

The Saudi Finance Minister scrambled backwards, flailing about on the bed, eyes wide in shock.

Oleg raised his gun and took off the red wig. "You scream, I guarantee you it will be your last surprise, *Essam*." The last word was streaked with sarcasm.

The Saudi's hands were clasped over his mouth in a pantomime suggesting he didn't trust himself not to scream. His wide eyes stared at the gun. The semi-clad Essam slowly nodded his compliance.

"Thank you for your cooperation."

The minister's head whipped around to see Bishop walking towards him from the bathroom. With the gun in his hand, he motioned to the robe.

"Dress yourself, please. It's not that kind of night."

"What… what do you want?"

There was terror in his eyes. How quickly his night had changed. Bishop found it impossible to care one iota.

It had taken little for him to convince the prostitute, whose name was Angelika, to disclose how the minister arranged his encounters. Then it was just a matter of Angelika impersonating her booking superior to arrange a replacement redhead. She told Essam that the substitute was rather shy, and asked if he would mind meeting her in another room on the same floor, quickly adding that as compensation for the earlier misunderstanding, there would be no charge for the evening. The minister eagerly accepted and it was quickly arranged.

Having noted which rooms were unoccupied, Bishop had negotiated with the front desk to use the one furthest from the minister's room and closest to the exits. In return for Angelika's assistance, Bishop had promised to speed up her visa application to the UK. It was a minor price to pay for access to the man who could give them Kali.

The Finance Minister whimpered, his gaze flicking between the two guns pointed at him.

"Hi there, mate." Bishop pressed the gun barrel into his forehead. "I'd recommend not moving again if you can help it. I've had a rough few days. To be perfectly honest, my nerves are a bit shot and I'm doped up on an amazing number of painkillers, so I'd avoid any sudden movements or impromptu noises if you can."

With a flop, Bishop sat on the bed, suddenly dizzy.

Oleg growled. "Are you alright?"

Not wanting to show weakness to either man, Bishop ignored the question. "You look good as a redhead."

"My mother was a redhead." Oleg crossed his arms.

"Did she have a three-day growth too?"

"Sometimes." Oleg sneered. "She did not always have time to shave because she was always out in the field lifting tractors or making goo goo eyes at pictures of Boris Yeltsin."

The minister sat up straight. "You will let me go. Now." He seemed to have recovered his composure. His accent was sprinkled with a British tone, no doubt from his elite-school upbringing. His face as hard as his words, he went on. "You do not realise who I am, the wrath I can bring upon you."

"No." Oleg stretched his arms. "You'll cooperate or we'll go down on you like a ton of bricks."

Bishop blinked several times. "We've talked about this. You leave the trash talking to me."

Face crinkled in confusion, Oleg shrugged. "What did I say?"

"It's come down on you like a ton of bricks. *Come* down."

"You told me not to use the word come." Oleg shook his head. "English is stupid."

The minister was unmoved by their chatter. He got to his feet and planted his fists on his hips, his air of arrogance now a fog. "Release me now and you shall not die, but I cannot promise it will not be unpleasant. Whatever misguided—"

He was silenced by the back of Bishop's hand being struck across his face. When he glanced up, blood flowed from the corner of his mouth.

Bishop leaned in. "Do you even know their names?"

"Whose names?" The minister pushed himself away as Bishop advanced, desperately searching for an escape. "What on earth are you talking about?"

"Those two servants you whipped to death. Do you know their names?"

The minister sneered. "Don't be absurd."

"Don't be absurd you know, or don't be absurd you wouldn't lower yourself to learn the names of the unwashed underlings you've killed?"

A slow veil of realisation descended over the minister's face. This wasn't an accident. This wasn't a misunderstanding. The men who held the guns knew exactly who he was and what he had done.

"What do you want?" All the arrogance had been stripped from his tone.

"Information." Bishop inspected the pistol in his hands. "That's all, Finance Minister. Just information. You give us what we require and you can be on your way. You won't be held for ransom or anything so mundane. You won't be killed. All you need to do is tell us about the shipment you purchased at the auction."

He drew back. "If I tell you about the shipment you may as well kill me. I'd be as good as dead. That I can guarantee."

"I'll tell you what I can guarantee, Minister." Bishop sighed. The gun in his hand seemed heavy. "You're alone, without your muscled henchmen. They won't know you're missing for hours. In those hours, you will be facing two determined armed men with an endless supply of pain-inflicting equipment and a lifetime of accumulated knowledge of every torture technique known to man. You can either die an agonising death or tell us what we want to know."

"You'll never get out of Marrakech alive."

"What happens to us is not your concern." Bishop pulled back the hammer of his pistol and aimed it at the minister's head. "You should really be concerned about your own welfare."

"You won't shoot me." The words were strong, but his eyes were filled with terror.

Bishop considered the gun in his hand. Frowning in agreement, he uncocked the pistol and tossed it on the far end of the bed. The minister watched the gun's arc. He wasn't looking when the first punch landed.

This was followed by a flurry of body blows, the final punch an uppercut that launched the minister from cowering on the bed and to being sprawled across the floor. Oleg sat up straight but didn't utter a word, watching the beating from afar but choosing not to interfere.

Huddled in the foetal position, the petrified man gazed up at his attacker. When Bishop approached, he scrambled backwards, whimpering.

Standing over him, Bishop sneered. "You're right. I won't shoot you. This is going to be far worse."

The blunt instrument cracked his knuckles and went to work.

CHAPTER TWELVE

The seatbelt sign lit up, indicating that the plane was about to begin its descent. Bishop awoke with a start after a thoroughly restful ten-minute sleep. He was unable to recall the last good night's sleep he'd had, or indeed, if he'd ever had one. He'd run out of pain medication somewhere near the equator.

Across the aisle, Oleg still slumbered in his first-class seat. The pilot's landing announcement was drowned out by the Russian's snoring. Bishop waved down a flight attendant and asked for a scotch.

Before boarding the plane, Bishop had contacted MI6. In the intervening few days, much had happened. The Pakistani Minister of Defence had been violently removed from office, probably due to the footage Bishop had supplied to MI6. There was no doubt the British government had traded the information, perhaps for some sort of military concession. It would have been a small price for Pakistan to pay for evidence of a traitor plotting a coup.

Paul reported that the information about Kali was finally falling into place. Illicit arms dealers were indeed disappearing or publicly retiring. One had turned herself in to the Spanish police. Betty Jo Anne Palfrey stated it was a pre-emptive move, given the state of her "profession". Then Paul added the kicker: on her way to the arraignment hearing, Palfrey's transport vehicle had inexplicably accelerated and careened off the Bac de Roda Bridge in Barcelona. There were no survivors.

While MI6 had been only mildly concerned with Kali before, that had turned into full-scale alarm. Paul mentioned that a member of cabinet had even spilt his tea —it was that serious. The tendrils of Kali spread wide, but until Bishop's official report, no head of the organisation had ever been identified. Now Interpol had a description and a target. Astrid may have eluded authorities in New York or Abu Dhabi, but Bishop doubted her luck would last.

The Saudi Finance Minister had been most helpful in providing the details of the third lot at the auction. The urgent collection of the Kali shipment was due to the fact that a Paraguayan rebel leader had purchased the shipment, then reneged on the deal at the last minute, unable to cough up the required five and a half million American dollars. The leader of the Paraguayan People's Liberation Army had been found flayed alive and nailed to a church door in San Pedro. Either Kali's debt collection was ruthless or the man had been a victim of the most extreme shaving accident in history.

The information gathered from bin Faisal had given them their only possible lead. The commercial airliner sped across the North Atlantic to make the rendezvous. They were cutting it fine. This was their one shot; they may never get another.

At least this time they wouldn't be alone. MI6 and SVR had launched a joint operation, a first in itself, to coordinate with Interpol. Everyone seemed to have forgotten the CIA's phone number. The Americans liked to think Haiti was their turf, but they weren't invited to this particular party.

The number of invitees already made Bishop nervous.

The more organisations, the more human beings aware of the operation, the greater the chance of being compromised. Temple and Astrid knew Bishop's real name, knew who he worked for. That meant they had ways of obtaining top-secret espionage information. The number of organisations involved was a risk. Then again, the melee they were about to enter could never be pulled off by two lone spies, especially when one was already walking wounded. And hardly walking at that. Hobbling wounded.

There couldn't be any screw-ups. On too many occasions Bishop had had the head of Kali within his grasp and she'd escaped unscathed. Not again.

Bishop glanced over at his snoring companion. During the long flight from Marrakech the two had hardly talked. At first they'd been preoccupied with coordinating efforts with their respective organisations, then consumed by the need for sleep. Bishop knew he was far from his prime, but it didn't matter. All he needed was to stay focused for the next six to twelve hours and then it would be over, one way or the other. This was the end game.

Checking coded communications from MI6, Bishop teetered from mildly confident to wholly despondent. Sensing that he was being watched, he turned to see Oleg staring at him.

Lifting an eyebrow, Bishop asked, "Spying on me again?"

"Again? That one time, Englishman."

"One's enough. Men have died for less." Bishop wasn't well rested.

"And it saved your life."

Bishop shrugged and swirled the ice in his glass. "Are your people in position?"

"Da. Yours?"

Bishop nodded. Conversation halted for several minutes, both men seemingly unwilling to engage in small talk. A flight attendant wearing far too much make-up served their first-class breakfast. Bishop hadn't even realised it was meant to be that time of day. He ordered another scotch.

Oleg nodded to the laptop beside him. "Our mutual friend has finally been reported missing."

In response, Bishop shrugged. *What is there to say?*

Oleg leaned over. "You were very convincing." His voice was low. "I almost believed you really would kill him. You are a persuasive liar."

With a tilt of his head, Bishop asked, "What made you think I was lying?"

That gave Oleg pause. They lapsed into silence again.

Essam bin Faisal would be found the following day; too late to halt their plans. An anonymous phone call would be made and a Saudi security team would be sent to one of the many seedy opium dens in the city. The minister would be high and loving life in the company of some ladies of the night. Given his track record, it wouldn't be out of character. He would, of course, claim to have been kidnapped and tortured. But besides the initial strike to the face, Bishop had been careful to leave no physical marks. With no supporting evidence and a history of womanising, it wouldn't be much of a stretch to believe the minister had simply spiralled out of control and succumbed to the evils the city of Marrakech provided in such abundance. At least, that was the plan.

Abducting a senior member of government and brutalising him mentally and physically was tantamount to a declaration of war. But the minister did not know who Oleg and Bishop were, nor who they worked for. It was as clean as they could manage with limited time and no support. They had done all they could to minimise the blowback; only time would tell how successful they'd been.

If the minister's presence at the auction was backed by the Saudi government, they would be furious at bin Faisal's failure to secure the delivery they'd paid millions for. If, on the other hand, he'd acted independently, he would face the wrath of Kali for divulging the location of the trade. If that was the case, there would be no place on earth he could hide from the retribution coming his way. Bishop held no sympathy for the man. While he wouldn't be the one to pull the trigger, he knew justice was coming for bin Faisal.

Bishop gazed out the window, but there was nothing to look at, just the North Atlantic Ocean as far as the eye could see. They would be landing in Miami soon, but that was only the first leg. They still had to catch a flight to Port-au-Prince, Haiti.

It wasn't a destination Bishop relished. Large swathes of the country were lawless, the government unstable and prone to corruption. It was a terrible place to run an operation, but it was perfect for an illegal arms deal.

What better way to elude scrutiny and the authorities than by choosing a country that had little of either? Haiti was as close to anarchy as you could find. Paying off prying eyes would be cheap. The challenge as Bishop saw it wasn't the legitimate government, it was the few dozen warlords who roamed the nearby lawless neighbourhoods. If they were to discover a major arms shipment in their midst, it would make one hell of an enticing target. The kinds of armaments the minister described would mean total dominance. It would mean taking out their rivals. Hell, it could mean taking the whole damn country.

During the interrogation, Bishop wondered why the Saudis would need that particular shipment. High-end assault weapons, grenade launchers, RPGs, tactical webbing and communications gear. This wasn't arming a few rebels with fourth-hand AK-47s. It was arming soldiers for a coup. And it had taken some persuasion, but that's exactly what the minister had admitted he was doing.

He, and possibly other senior members of the government, were playing a high-stakes game of Russian roulette. In recent years the royal family, while still loved and respected, had faced challenges from within their country. A group had sprung up, Huriya, or Freedom. They, as the name suggested, were demanding more freedom, threatening open rebellion, and challenges to authority were on the rise. Staging a mini rebellion within their borders would bring the troublemakers to the surface, like drawing poison from a wound. At the eleventh hour the leaders of the coup would be taken down from within—crisis averted. It was unbelievably risky. The intention was to bolster public opinion and have the masses rally around their sovereign and their government.

Towards the end of the interrogation the minister had become delirious, and it had been increasingly difficult to understand his pained ramblings. It was unclear if he was working alone or under the direction of his government.

Bishop thumped the armrest. He had to stop with the speculation. The role of the spy wasn't to understand the machinations of history, it was to be the silent weapon of their country, used to maintain the status quo or break it apart. Theirs was not to reason why, theirs was to do or die. Although Bishop preferred Minogue over Tennyson.

Whatever the minister's motivation, tens of thousands would have died for the man's manipulation of public opinion. Again, Bishop cared little that bin Faisal's time on the planet was limited.

At the very least, Bishop and Oleg had averted an international crisis. Now they were aiming to take down those who had fanned it. Kali would be trading the shipment for cash—US dollars, to be precise. MI6 reported that an unscheduled flight from Saudi Arabia had landed hours before. The deal was going down; they had to be in position to capture as many as possible. This was their one chance to catch Kali in the act.

The location of the trade was the Port International de Port-au-Prince, the seaport of the Haitian capital. Part government run, part private, it was large enough for a major shipment of arms, small enough to elude scrutiny. Interpol had decided it best to make the arrests at the Haitian end. It was deemed the Haitian authorities were less likely to kick up an international stink than if they'd tried to make an arrest on royal Saudi soil.

The two men currently in first class were mere observers, their work officially done. At least, that was what Bishop's superiors believed. Interpol, MI6, SVR and the Haitian police would have more than enough resources to intercept the trade and arrest those responsible.

Running his fingers down the fresh scar on his side, Bishop closed his eyes and forced himself to rest. He needed all the energy his battered body could generate. Only one target interested him. If that target was in Haiti, all the forces combined wouldn't prevent Bishop from extracting his revenge.

Oleg put down his binoculars in frustration. "This is going to end very badly."

They sat in the cramped cabin of a crane high above the Port International. They were slowly roasting in the stifling conditions. The earlier humidity had given way to an uncomfortable dry heat. The window was open, but did little to prevent them baking in their own sweat. The cabin gently swayed in the warm wind. Far below, half a dozen MI6 and SVR agents, three Interpol representatives straight from Buenos Aires and twenty members of para-military units of the Haitian National Police were moving into final positions.

"You think?"

Oleg gave him a sideways glance. "Yes… that is why I said it."

"No, it's a saying for… yes, it's going to end badly. This is what happens when you organise tactical assaults by committee, you get a camel."

"There's a camel?" Oleg picked up the binoculars and examined the landscape below. "Why do they need a camel?"

"No… we need to work on your idioms. A camel is a horse designed by committee. It's a saying."

"It's not a very good saying." Oleg put the binoculars down. "Why do they always have animals? A bird in the hand is worth two in the bush. Why do you want a bird in your hands? They flap and shit everywhere. Stay in the bush, what do I care?"

"You're rather literal."

"I am Russian. We are a practical people. We have no time for trivialities."

Bishop decided to leave the conversation there. On the ground, whatever committee had organised the operation had botched it. The deployment throughout the port facility was too haphazard. There were too many gaps, while other areas had overlaps of personnel, which would cause problems of their own.

Both Oleg and Bishop had headsets to coordinate their own countrymen. They were the link between the two spy agencies. There was no way to contact Interpol or the Haitians. That concerned Bishop. Without proper comms, groups could be caught in friendly crossfire or backed into kill zones. He was glad he was far above the firefight because it could descend into a shitshow in no time at all. It would take a minor miracle for the operation not to end in a bloodbath.

The Cambodian-registered ship *Aurora* was anchored at the second berth. It was a flag-of-convenience ship of vague ownership. A Saudi tanker returning from the Port of New York and New Jersey had conveniently reported mechanical problems and was en route, scheduled to arrive in a day's time. A port facilities storage shed had been hired by an untraceable Cayman Islands firm, coincidentally for two days. It was all rather neat, with submissible evidence. If they wanted witnesses, their forces on the ground should do their best to avoid a massacre.

Worse, if a single one of the targets got away they would alert the Saudi ship and the case could easily fall apart, leaving nothing to tie the deal to the Saudis. Interpol believed the best chance of success was to intercept the deal as it was being done. Bishop was cynical, but the decision had been made before he arrived.

Oleg and Bishop waited. Sweated and waited. There was nothing left for them to coordinate. Half an hour passed with no major movement on the ground. The tedium wore down Bishop's focus like a nail file.

Oleg broke the silence. "Are Hall & Oates English?"

"Who?" Bishop didn't recall any operatives by those names.

"The musical group." Oleg's eyes were still focused on the ground far below. "Are they English?"

Thinking he was being wound up, Bishop replied, "No, they're American. Why on earth did you ask me that?"

"Oh. They're very good."

"I'm waiting for the joke."

"No joke." Oleg turned to him. "I like them very much, I was just wondering."

They lapsed into silence again. Beneath them, nothing moved bar the occasional forklift. The sun continued to beat down.

Five minutes later, Bishop sighed loudly. "Now I bloody have 'Maneater' in my head."

"Oh, that's a great one! *Ooh here she comes, watch out boys she'll chew you up!* Excellent."

Bishop smirked and shook his head. "You're a weird unit, Oleg."

Are we friends now? Bishop wondered to himself. Did he trust the Russian? The answer was probably still no, though he had saved Bishop on more than one occasion. They worked well as a team. But friends? There were few people Bishop held in that category. Calling Oleg a friend was a stretch. Begrudging associates would be more accurate. It was unlikely they would be exchanging Christmas cards and holidaying by the Black Sea anytime soon.

Bringing his meandering mind back to the reason they were on the swaying crane, Oleg nudged him and nodded towards an area on the dock to the west.

"What is this fool doing?"

On the ground, a young Haitian officer had taken up position. He was splayed on the ground, machine gun pointed at the causeway leading to the designated exchange point. Not only was his back fully exposed to two buildings with windows facing his way, but he had chosen a spot surrounded by oil barrels and dilapidated fuel pumps. He may as well have been sitting on a stack of dynamite smoking a cigar.

"Perhaps this crane is not as far away as it could have been?"

Taking a closer look through the binoculars, Bishop sighed. "I think you're right."

It was too late to move. He checked his watch. It had taken ten minutes to climb up the crane and take their position. If they relocated themselves now it would be all over by the time they reached the ground. Bishop hoped the kid by the fuel station was a better shot than he was a tactician.

Bishop called through the warning to his people; Oleg did the same. Their agents were better hidden. The SVR people were disguised as dock workers in grubby over-alls and hats. The MI6 agents were in a tiny shed with long-range weapons. Bishop was satisfied they'd be even more cooked in their hiding place than he was.

The Haitian police were poorly concealed throughout the docks, and would be the ones making the actual arrests. The Interpol representatives were hidden in a nearby portable office, ready to spring out after the fact and take all the credit.

On the ground a wind sock on one of the customs buildings hardly moved. Up high, the crane felt like one of those inflatable flailing tube men. Bishop had never had a problem with heights, but the crane made him uneasy. He'd seen the rust on the long trek up.

The port itself was small, with a handful of berths and few places to hide. The trade itself was to take place on a small island connected to the south pier. The causeway linking the island to the main port would be where the Haitians would make the intercept, cutting off the money men and the representatives of Kali from escape.

Oleg nudged Bishop to follow his line of sight. A white Range Rover crept through the unmanned front gates of the port. From what Bishop could see, four men sat in the car, heads darting around nervously. The money had arrived.

"Here we go."

Using their headsets, both men gave their teams a heads-up. The deal was going down.

All eyes were on the SUV or on the island where the exchange was to take place. All eyes, that is, except Bishop's. His job of informing his fellow MI6 agents done, he had a new role. An unauthorised one. He wasn't concerned with the location of the trade. He concentrated on the periphery. The shadows. The places where spiders hid. He was searching for an assassin.

The white SUV rolled towards the end of the causeway, double parking next to a rusted shipping container. The four men exited and glanced around nervously. Fifty metres away, six men emerged from the shadows on the island.

One of the men who'd stepped out of the SUV carried a large suitcase. The specified $5.8 million untraceable US dollars. There would be few people in this poor nation who wouldn't kill a loved one to get their hands on that kind of money. The man clutching it to his chest seemed to understand this. Through the binoculars Bishop saw the torrents of perspiration cascading down his face. If he wasn't shot in the next five minutes he'd surely drown in his own sweat.

The four stepped onto the start of the causeway cautiously. The six men they were meeting stood unmoving ahead of them, machine guns slung across their backs. Every muscle Bishop possessed was tense. Beside him, Oleg remained as still as a headstone. They needed everyone to keep their cool until the deal was done. It would take luck, but if everyone kept their heads, they'd still be breathing at the end of the day.

As if hearing Bishop's optimistic thoughts, a battered police van sped through the port gates and barrelled towards the causeway. It skidded to a halt and a dozen Haitian police officers bailed out, guns raised.

Bishop's fist slammed into the metal floor. "Too soon. Too fucking soon!"

The deal hadn't been made. The Haitians had blown their load too early. Everyone on the ground was about to be involved in a bloodbath.

Oleg and Bishop screamed orders into their headsets. The moneymen spun around in circles, unsure where to run, but the six armed Kali guards knew exactly what to do. They raised their guns and fired.

Hell was loosed upon Haiti.

CHAPTER THIRTEEN

Bishop's stomach churned at the pure chaotic madness that unfolded far below. The distance from the fighting made Bishop's assessment more clinical, but the horrifying events were no less real.

The Kali fighters and the Haitian police exchanged frenzied gunfire. The Saudis were caught in the middle. Within seconds two white-thobed Saudis were pockmarked red and fell. The other two sprinted for the apparent safety of the water. Only one made it. The taller one received a barrage in the back and fell to the road, dead, while the other dove into the murky water of the port.

The Kali and Haitian forces fired unrelenting barrages at one another, whether from bloodthirstiness or fear of not fighting hard enough, Bishop was unsure. The smart ones found cover or dropped to the ground. Others fell where they stood. Several Haitians fell backwards, bullets ripping the life from their young bodies. The Kali troops were far more trained and disciplined. Without orders, they rotated their fire, allowing their team members to reload. They were methodical, and within seconds they had whittled down the Haitian force, taking minimal casualties. In other circumstances, Bishop would have been impressed. They must be ex-Special Forces. At the end of the firefight, all six remained standing, with only two receiving minor injuries.

It wasn't over yet.

The hidden Haitian police emerged, firing on the Kali forces. If they were as undisciplined as their compatriots, they would soon be joining the mounting piles of dead. It was the small number of spies who would be the ones to inflict damage. High above the melee Bishop and Oleg coordinated their forces. Attack vectors were limited, but their combined forces had a skill set the others lacked: patience, advanced weaponry and battle experience.

Bishop ordered them to engage. They did exactly that. Poking weapons through windows, the MI6 agents fired their high-powered firearms. The first Kali fighter fell, a giant hole where his chest used to be. Another turned to run, but his head detonated in an explosion of gore.

"Keep at least one alive, you bastards."

Bishop's tone was half camaraderie, half exasperation. The deal had descended into a cluster fuck faster than anyone had feared. They needed arms dealers to tie it all to Kali. The dead made poor witnesses.

Something was concerning Bishop. The Kali fighters backed away slowly to the island connected to the causeway. Strategically, it was suicidal. There was nothing beyond the island but water. The Haitian navy had two patrol boats closing in. They were cut off.

"Why choose that place for the deal?"

Oleg turned to him. "It is out of the way?"

Realising he'd started a conversation by mistake, Bishop replied, "Yes, but why there? Surely any suffi-ciently trained soldier has contingencies? They've painted themselves into a corner. There's no way out. Unless…"

Bishop's binoculars flung to the corners of the port, searching any half-reasonable position to set up a sniper's nest. Unable to see anything out of the ordinary, he swivelled his view to the kid by the fuel pump. His hands were flopped at an unnatural angle, his thin body slumped over his weapon. Puffs of dirt erupted near the police officer's head.

"She's going to blow the fuel."

"Who is?"

Before he could answer, a giant orange and black fire-ball erupted into the sky.

Kali had blown the fuel depot. They had their distraction. On the ground, people scattered like bugs under a lifted rock, scurrying in all directions. Chaos reigned. The remaining Haitian police dropped where they stood, succumbing to sniper's bullets. Bishop was willing to put good money on who the sniper was.

Performing urgent mental gymnastics to triangulate Astrid's position, Bishop pitched his binoculars around the dock. Beside him, Oleg was pointing and yelling at his comrades in Russian. Bishop did the same. Nobody had a target.

The first SVR agent cried out, then the second. Urgent calls went unanswered. Bishop screamed at his men to take cover. It was too late.

An RPG spewed smoke as it snaked its way towards the MI6 shed.

"Get out!"

Bishop's call came too late. The small tin shed erupted in a fireball, sending shrapnel and debris in all directions. All that remained was a smoking ruin. The men and women he had just met were dead, never to return to their families. It was a horrific, inhumane way to die. He would mourn his colleagues later. They were professionals, they'd want him to stay on mission. Grieving would come, but right now he had more immediate concerns.

"Where's the money?"

Oleg's head swivelled towards him. "What?"

"The case, with the money. Where is it?"

There was no sign of the case on the causeway.

"Our countrymen are dead!" Oleg's tone was hard; he was astonished at Bishop's heartless observation.

"The case is gone. Either Kali has more people on the ground or one of the Haitians got greedy. I think the former."

"Whatever. We have more pressing matters."

Oleg nodded towards the devastation below. Thrashing, smoking bodies; silent screams. Motionless forms, never to move again. Doing his best to ignore the human cost, Bishop focused on what he had to do next. The RPG had left a trail. A trail that led to a decrepit tugboat moored to a tiny pier. It was a trail that led to Astrid. Bishop picked up his pistol.

Yanking open the trapdoor on the floor of the cabin, Bishop checked the rounds of his Glock and slapped the magazine in place.

"You'll never get to the ground in time." Oleg's tone was even. Bishop was unsure if it was due to the death of his comrades or in response to Bishop's action.

Oleg was right. It had taken them over ten minutes to climb the crane. The descent would be quicker, but even so, Astrid would be long gone by the time he reached the ground. Then a thought struck him. Bishop beamed.

"Who said I was going to climb down?"

Forehead creased in confusion, Oleg shook his head. He followed Bishop's eyes to the end of the crane. Then he understood. "You are without a doubt the most insane human being I have ever met."

The MI6 agent bowed slightly. "I'll take that as a compliment."

"It was not meant as one."

Bishop waggled his eyebrows. "I know."

Moments later he was high above the sun-baked earth on all fours, crawling across the arm of the crane. His hair fluttered in the heavy breeze. Hand over hand, he clung to the crane for dear life, doing his best to imagine that it was merely feet off the ground. He made steady but slow progress. Suddenly a gust of wind buffeted Bishop and shunted him to the left, and his handhold slipped. Recovering, he sucked in a deep breath.

"What the fuck was I thinking?"

Over the headset came the reply. "Would you like me to sing to you again?"

Bishop inched forward. "You do and I'll jump."

"I am still undecided if I should sing or not."

Far below, no one had exited the tugboat. The occasional writhing body had been ruthlessly taken out by the sniper at the front of the boat. Oleg had tried to raise the Haitian police but couldn't get through. Either their communications were down or the signal was being blocked.

Mouth dry, Bishop finally reached the end of the crane. Now came the hard bit.

"Hoist it up."

As instructed, Oleg retracted the crane. At the very end was a large hook, about half a metre in size, and above that was a metal ball about the size of his head. In theory, all Bishop had to do was drop from the end of the crane onto the ball, then place his foot in the hook and wait to be be lowered to the ground. In theory. Below that little leap was 100 metres of certain death. If he slipped, if he lost his grip for even an instant there would be no second chances. Bishop would fall, clawing at the air while screaming the best profanities His Majesty's language had to offer.

Inhaling deeply, Bishop leapt from the crane. His foot hit the ball and it moved far more than he'd expected. He lost his footing. Gritting his teeth, his left hand reached out to grasp the chain. He missed. Bishop was in freefall. Below was nothing but ground. In a desperate lunge, his right hand grabbed at the rapidly disappearing hook. His fingers barely gripped the rusted metal, but miraculously they held for a fraction of a second. Carefully, he raised his left hand to take a more secure hold. He got hold of the hook and held fast.

In seconds he pulled himself up. All those push-ups and chin-ups paid off. He planted his foot securely in the hook and glanced up at the crane's cabin.

"Okay, let's go."

The motor whirred and the hook descended towards the ground.

"You almost died."

"Thank you for letting me know, I completely missed it." For the first time, Bishop was aware of his breathing. "I think after this I might retire and run a flower shop."

"Know anything about flowers?"

"Not a thing."

"It's a well thought-out plan, then."

Bishop looked down and gritted his teeth. "Much like this one really. Seems to be a recurring theme."

The hook descended rapidly, but as he dropped lower, Bishop realised it would be out of range of the tugboat unless he did something about it.

Into the headset, Bishop growled, "I want you to swing this baby like Sinatra at the Sands."

Silence followed. Eventually, Oleg replied, "I have absolutely no idea what that means."

"Swing me around in an arc, it's the only way I'm

going to reach the boat. Otherwise I'll need to cross open ground and I'll never make it."

On the ground, all remained still apart from sporadic bursts of gunfire quickly quashed by sniper's bullets. Nobody had emerged from the tugboat.

Bishop heard the clunk of levers. "I see. And where does Sinatra come in?"

The crane groaned and the huge arm began to move in a slow arc. The wire Bishop dangled from swayed and dragged him to the left. In no time, he was fighting to hang on as the hook spun around and the ground became a swirling blur. A blur that was steadily growing closer.

"Get ready." Oleg's voice was hurried. "Next round you'll reach the boat."

The world was a smear. Bishop only knew which way was up because the upper part was blue. He clung to the wire for dear life. It was nearly at right angles to the ground. He had no idea how he was meant to dismount the swirling chaos of the crane to confront the enemy on the tugboat. The speed was ludicrous. He'd envisaged himself swinging in, gun blazing, like Errol Flynn—if Errol Flynn was prone to firing Glocks at clandestine international arms dealing syndicates while swinging on a crane. It was practically the same. But now, the thought of letting go of the end of the crane filled him with mounting dread and the certainty of a crushed skull.

"Three."

"I'm not ready."

"Two."

"Oleg… I…"

"Now, Bishop!"

The tugboat came at Bishop like a freight train. In an instant he was committed, he had no choice. It was either leap or slam into the hull and be squashed like a bug.

Bishop leapt.

Time slowed. In midair, Bishop extracted the pistol from the rear of his pants. Behind him, the hook caught on the hawsehole on the bow and came to an abrupt halt. Bishop didn't.

Flying through the air, he was hurled over the deck. Spinning head over heels, Bishop attempted to control his landing, but it was too late. He hit the deck hard, face forward, arms protecting his head, then scrunched into a ball and tumbled uncontrollably. Splaying his body, he tried to slow himself down as he hurtled across the deck.

Decelerating enough to gather his wits, he ignored his screaming body. Bishop stood and realised the pistol was no longer in his hands. He forced his watery eyes to focus.

"Looking for this?"

Bishop reluctantly turned to see a grey-hooded woman in the doorway of the wheelhouse on the deck above him. In one hand she held his Glock, in the other, a silenced Beretta M9A3. Both were pointed at Bishop.

"Thanks ever so much. I've been searching every-where for it. It's always the last place you look, isn't it?"

There were several metres and a ladder between them. Astrid was too high for him to reach in one leap. She was out of range, had the high ground and had him severely outgunned.

"I suppose I have you to thank for all this?" Astrid jerked her head towards the smoking ruins of the port.

"No. I'm reasonably certain I wasn't the one firing off RPGs and killing indiscriminately."

Bishop's back was aflame and each intake of air felt like an insurmountable hurdle, but he would not give the woman the satisfaction of showing weakness. Not now. Not ever.

Astrid snorted. "Oh, don't be so obtuse."

"I always thought I was rather acute."

Astrid blinked several times. "Did you just try to make a geometry joke?"

"I sometimes talk in circles, but I didn't see the point." Bishop shrugged. "Sorry, I was off on a tangent."

She pointed the Beretta at his head. "Please stop."

Bishop's expression turned dark, his voice like stone. "Surrender. You won't make it out of here alive if you don't, Astrid."

She raised an eyebrow. "I seem to have done alright so far. Plus," she glanced down at him, "I seem to be the one holding the guns. Obviously, I'm no expert on these things, but I'd say you're the one who's not making it out alive." Astrid waved the guns, gesturing for Bishop to step back, then descended the ladder and stepped onto the deck. "You can't charm the pants off me now."

"They are very nice pants."

"You hate me, don't you Bishop?"

"You have no idea."

"Perhaps." Astrid studied the pistol in her hand. "Hate. It's an exquisite emotion. So passionate. So intense. Isn't it?" Her smile blazed at him. "I hate you too, Bishop. We hate each other so much. Who hates the most, I wonder? You, maybe? I think you hate me so much you're going to die from it."

"One of us will, I assure you."

"That's where you're wrong." Astrid leaned forward, pointing the barrel at his forehead. It wasn't the first time she'd aimed his own pistol at him. "You're going to die, Charles Bishop."

Bishop tapped the side of his head. "Now."

Astrid baulked slightly. "Did you just ask me to kill you?"

Bishop raised an eyebrow. "I wasn't talking to you."

The entire tugboat groaned. The sound of grinding metal was deafening. The world tilted on its axis as the bow of the boat lifted from the murky waters of the port and lurched skyward.

Oleg had understood the message and retracted the crane's hook, tugboat and all. Moorings snapped, water surged, the world twisted. Bishop leapt across and grabbed the boat's railing, threading his arm through the rope tied to the tyres on the side of the lurching boat.

Astrid, at the centre of the deck, was nowhere near anything to hold onto. As the heavy vessel violently drew vertical she lost her footing and stumbled. Her feet searched for ground but found only air. She toppled downward, towards the wheelhouse, which was now the floor.

She landed on her back, hitting with a hard "Oof".

Bishop's Glock sailed downward towards the rapidly disappearing earth. Her silenced pistol spilled from her hand and skidded across the wood. Astrid blinked several times, stunned.

The tugboat creaked as it swayed in the wind, and the ground grew more distant by the second. Bishop only had a moment. If Astrid recovered and picked up the gun, he'd have no defence. The distance between the railing and the wheelhouse was only a few metres, but if he mistimed his leap he'd hurtle towards terra firma and death. It was a theme he was growing far too accustomed to. Bishop gritted his teeth and leapt.

Landing awkwardly, his ankle felt like it had been smashed by a sledgehammer. Falling on his side, Bishop scrambled towards the Beretta. Astrid wasn't as stunned as he first thought; she hoisted herself up to clamber towards the gun.

But she was too slow.

Bishop picked up the Beretta and pulled back the hammer. "Don't."

Eyes crazed, Astrid leapt towards him, fingernails

raised like claws. She thrashed at him wildly. Bishop ducked and threw a Kizami-Zuki karate jab to her ribs. It threw her off balance. Staggering, she took another swing as she tried to find her footing, but there was nowhere to step. Astrid fell off the wheelhouse, grasping at air, and plummeted to the earth.

Dropping to his chest, Bishop shot out his hand and grabbed Astrid's wrist. They both grunted as she jerked to halt. With a heave, he hoisted her upward until she could clamber up of her own volition. When she was back on the wheelhouse, she eyed the gun on the other side of him.

Bishop's lips curled into a sneer. "Seriously? I wouldn't advise it."

Astrid grunted and collapsed backwards, knowing it was futile. She winced and closed her eyes, defeated.

There were no thanks for saving her life. Not that he expected any.

It would be easy to advise Paul and the other MI6 superiors that he'd saved Astrid because she had vital information that would facilitate the apprehension of the Kali organisation. But Bishop knew it wasn't entirely true. He would spend time with his therapist over that one, but for now, there were more pressing matters.

"Oleg," Bishop wheezed, "if there's anyone left alive down there, please inform them that we have the leader of Kali in custody." He looked at the face he had once considered so beautiful. "If you could lower us anytime soon, that would be splendid. The sooner this woman is out of my sight, the better."

"Look at the big hero." Astrid's voice was as cold as a mortician's slab. "Wins the day *and* gets the girl. My, they'll probably give you a medal or a sash of some description, won't they? You must feel very special."

"The only thing I feel is tired."

"You do seem tired. Maybe lie down. I could hold the gun for you. Looks heavy."

The tugboat halted its ascent with a shunt. Seconds later it reversed and slowly headed towards terra firma once more.

Astrid's face changed again. She appeared more angelic. On the outside. "You haven't changed anything, you know? You can take me down, but nothing will change."

"I don't know about that. A man can change the world with an opportunity and one bullet." She slithered towards him. In response, Bishop aimed the pistol at her. "Don't give me an opportunity, Astrid."

The head of Kali slumped backwards and huffed. The tugboat descended. Bishop just wanted a scotch, and to lie down for a year or two.

CHAPTER FOURTEEN

The white van clattered so much that Bishop's teeth rattled. He was beginning to wonder if the driver wasn't deliberately aiming for the potholes. In the back of the Haitian police van, Bishop sat on a bench opposite a serene-looking Astrid. Her demeanour was in direct contrast to the chaos she'd wrought. The Haitians had suffered terrible losses. There were no survivors from the Saudi side. There were Kali dead too, but not all members on the ground were accounted for.

The back of the van had no windows, only the white metal walls. Beside them were two police officers barely old enough to shave. They formed part of the second wave of police after their comrades had been brutally eliminated by Astrid and her cohorts. There had been a brief period where the police had wanted to execute her on the spot. Calmer heads had prevailed.

Those left in authority, Bishop included, thought it best to take no chances and get Astrid out of the country ASAP. They were headed straight for the airport. Well, almost straight. The police were travelling in a wide arc, avoiding one neighbourhood in particular.

Cité Soleil was an infamous part of Port-au-Prince, situated between the port and the airport. The UN called Cité Soleil the most dangerous place on earth. Bishop thought it was an understatement. Armed gangs roamed the streets and terrorised the neighbourhood. Murder, rape, kidnapping and shootings were still common, as was lynching. The government sporadically attempted to remind the populous lynching was a crime but they continue on anyway.

The neighbourhood was continually terrorised by armed gangs who had driven the police out in the nineties. They never returned. In 2007 UN troops aided by heavily armed Haitian police were sent into Cité Soleil. Four lives were lost and another ten were injured. They lasted one hour. All in all, Bishop would prefer Cirque du Soleil.

He was thankful the police had decided the direct route was not a viable option. It meant the trip was longer, but at least they would be alive by the end of it. The van hit another pothole and Bishop nearly hit his head on the roof. Astrid grinned in amusement.

He did his best to ignore her beauty. It had been insane for him to think about falling for this woman. He had thawed the ice cap of his soul for her and had paid a hefty price for it. Bishop felt the ice cap freezing over once more, likely for the last time.

Tilting her head, she beamed pleasantly. "You could have let me fall to my death. Don't get me wrong, I'm grateful, but I'm wondering why you saved me?"

"What can I say? I was momentarily overcome with sentimentality." The edges of Bishop's mouth hardened. "The moment has passed."

Astrid's eyes lit up. "I do so like being quoted, it makes me feel important."

"You may have been once, but no longer. Soon you'll

just be a prisoner with a number. You'd best get used to it."

"You could let me go." She waggled her shoulders and did a convincing imitation of an innocent angel.

Bishop let loose a hearty laugh. "I could. But it's more likely this van will turn into a flying unicorn."

Astrid smirked. "Would we still be in the van when it turned into a unicorn? Because eww."

Bishop offered no reply.

She shrugged amiably. "It's a shame, really, that you and I didn't meet in different circumstances." Bishop scoffed, but she went on. "No, I honestly mean it. We're cut from the same cloth, you and me. You feel it, I know you do."

"Are you trying to charm me? Really? You remember the stabbing?" Bishop made a motion to emphasise the point. "You stabbed me. You sliced me like a grapefruit. I have many fond memories in life: my first teenage love, firing my first gun, getting the job at MI6, those triplets in Belize, but I assure you, my good woman, your torture wasn't one of them."

"Oh, you know what I mean. You can't say we didn't have chemistry. Even knowing who you were, who you represented, I couldn't bring myself to end you."

"Bullshit." Bishop was angry now. He did his best to keep the venom from his tone. "In that torture chamber I was close to death and you wanted to see how long I could last. Don't turn your sadistic torture into some romantic gesture. It's like a rhino trying to mate with a chihuahua—it just doesn't fit."

With a shrug, Astrid inspected the filthy floor. "If that's what you want to believe, fine. All I know is truth. In spite of the roles we were playing, we *connected*. You felt it, I know you did."

There was no way Bishop would confirm it. He would

never give her the satisfaction. Before he knew the truth about her, he had broken many rules for Astrid. There'd been an enigmatic quality about the woman that made him challenge his own beliefs and play loose with the tenets of his profession. He rubbed the fresh scar on his side. It still twinged.

"I'm truly am sorry we didn't meet in a different part of our lives, Charles Bishop."

The woman was mad. Completely and utterly insane. *She had to be, surely?* Did she honestly believe that a smattering of nice words meant Bishop would let her go with a fond farewell and a packed lunch? Notwithstanding the tiny, insignificant fragment of attraction that remained, he knew her true self, the utter blackness of her soul. Somehow, after all that had happened, she seemed to genuinely believe they still had a connection. Was she completely delusional or a convincing actor? Bishop was too tired to know and too jaded to care. Soon Astrid would no longer be his concern.

In reply to her question, Bishop slipped into a stony silence. It only amplified the noise of a revving engine outside. Someone was apparently incapable of riding their motorbike without throttling the hell out of it.

"For what it's worth, Charles, I'm truly sorry."

Bishop's face creased in confusion. "For what?"

Astrid gripped her seat tight. "This."

Something unseen *clanged* loudly against the side of the van. It was followed by another on the other side. They were being attacked. Gunfire erupted from all flanks. Unable to see what was going on, Bishop extracted his pistol. The two petrified police officers did the same, pistols shaking in their hands. Astrid seemed entertained.

Bishop wished there were windows so he could see what was going on. Urgent shouts erupted from everywhere. The van sped up, seemingly trying to outrun their foes. More shouts, more gunfire. An explosion rocked the van, sloping everything sideways. They'd blown a tyre and the van fishtailed wildly.

Bishop turned to the driver's cabin and yelled, "Don't brake!"

The driver braked.

The officer at the wheel clearly didn't know not to apply brakes with a blown tyre. The van spun, and all four in the back were flung around like washing in a machine. Bishop kept Astrid at bay with his boot, not wanting her to get close to him or his weapon.

With a deafening *crash*, the van shuddered and rocked so much it nearly toppled over, before landing the right way up with a thud. A burst of gunfire coupled with the sounds of smashing glass and brief screams of pain told Bishop that the driver and his offsider were dead.

Blood ran from a cut on Astrid's cheek. Under his boot, she smiled. "You should have let me go when you had the chance."

More automatic fire and agonised screams. Then silence. That was worse. Silence meant Bishop didn't know where he stood, what was happening or what his next move should be.

The rear of the van erupted in a blinding explosion. Unable to see anything, Bishop waited for a bullet. None came. Perhaps it was the boot wedged on their boss's neck and the gun barrel aimed at her forehead.

Smoke cleared and Bishop could see better. The two police lay facedown on the van's floor, their guns cold, having never been fired. Three muscled men and two equally intimidating women in camouflage fatigues aimed multiple weapons at Bishop.

"Is this my Uber Eats order? Please tell me you remembered the extra salad dressing this time."

"Give up, Bishop, it's over." Astrid glared at him.

"I'm sorry, I couldn't hear you over the sound of this Beretta in your face."

"You need to let me go. You have my word you'll be set free. You don't let me go, you'll be dead within the minute."

"You'll kill me anyway."

"I just said I'd let you go."

"You'll forgive me if I'm somewhat sceptical about your honesty in this and all matters."

Astrid sniffed. "You have a choice." She lifted a palm. "Certain death." She lifted the other palm so her hands were either side of his gun. "Or the possibility of living. The odds you want to attach to that are up to you, but they're certainly higher than zero. Let me go, Charles. You might see out the day, maybe find those triplets in Belize." Her face turned cold. "You have three seconds."

A burning pit of anger welled deep inside him. Anger at not taking the right precautions in escorting the head of Kali. Anger at the situation he had been forced into. Anger at more lives lost. But most of all, anger at Astrid. This should have been over. She shouldn't have the upper hand yet again. The woman was as formidable as she was wicked. He couldn't let her win.

Grinding his teeth, Bishop furiously buried the gun barrel further into her skull. A simple twitch of his finger would cause it all to end. It would be final. It would be quick. An elegant solution to a complex problem.

But no.

Bishop eased off, released the hammer, took his finger from the trigger and held the Beretta skyward, disarmed. He took his boot off Astrid and she exhaled deeply. Snatching the weapon from him, she brushed past him wordlessly.

It wasn't chivalry that spared her life. Nor was it the

fear of sacrificing himself for King and Country. It was pure bloody-mindedness. Astrid needed to be held accountable for her crimes, to aid in the dismantling of her arms empire. Someone had to haul her treacherous arse into a court of law.

Bishop had no illusions about the worth of her word. He just hoped for a quick death. A warrior's death; one worthy of such a blunt instrument. Since entering the espionage business Bishop had known his fate would not be to grow old and die lying in his own shit in a retirement home for elderly spies. He always knew his fate would come far sooner. And be more brutal.

He turned to Astrid. "Let's get it over with."

After a brief conversation with her saviours, Astrid turned to him, stone faced. "You spared my life. I'll spare yours."

"My, how gracious of you."

Her face turned positively angelic. Astrid beamed. "You're right, *I am* very gracious."

Astrid pivoted and kicked Bishop in the thigh, right where she'd shot him the first time. "A little graciousness."

The pain was excruciating. In agony, Bishop smacked the rear of his skull on the van's floor. His hands darted to the wound. It hurt like a bitch.

Astrid leaned over him, chuckling. "Okay, not *that* gracious."

Through clenched teeth, Bishop yelled, "Stop wounding me, woman."

"Stop giving me the chance." Astrid's face turned cold as arctic snow. "If I see you again, I will kill you Charles Bishop."

"I have absolutely no doubt."

With swift hand gestures, Astrid issued orders to her crew and they headed towards the waiting Range Rover.

Curious locals were kept at bay by stern expressions and sweeping weapons.

The looks the locals gave Bishop varied. Some watched him with pity, many were curious, others glared at him with nothing short of outright anger. The police van had a broken axle and was undrivable. Walking back to port in his condition seemed an insurmountable task.

Raising his voice as Astrid walked away, Bishop said, "You saved my life and you're leaving me here?"

Astrid turned and looked at the gathering crowd, a smirk creasing her flawless features. She turned to him. "Surely a man of your resourcefulness can figure it out?"

"Oh, certainly." Bishop's bravado was as genuine as a twenty-dollar Rolex. "I only meant you could have made it more difficult."

With a sweet laugh, Astrid shook her head. "Maybe I will."

A severe-looking woman with short, dyed blonde hair checked her watch. "We have thirty minutes before your flight starts boarding."

Astrid nodded and slid into the rear of the vehicle. Before she slammed the door, she turned to Bishop and blew him a kiss. The SUV revved its engine and sped away.

Scrambling across the grimy floor, Bishop checked the two police officers for a pulse. The effort was futile; Astrid's troops had been brutally efficient. One had a baton on his belt, Bishop grabbed it as the officer would no longer need it. The van wasn't going anywhere either. He would need another way out.

Curious faces appeared around the periphery of the van. Bishop didn't believe every resident of Cité Soleil was a vicious murderous thug, but that didn't mean the gun battle hadn't attracted some of the worst elements. He was most likely situated near the edge of the neighbourhood, and had no idea if these people meant him harm or were there to help. Bishop gripped the baton tight, just in case.

The sound of a vehicle approaching sent the locals scattering. Bishop couldn't see the car, but heard the screech of tyres. A lone figure exited and walked towards the back of the van. He had a submachinegun and a serious disposition.

Eying the baton in Bishop's hand, Oleg asked, "Are you going to beat me off?"

"Seriously man, I'm yet to be convinced you're not doing that on purpose."

He quickly brought Oleg up to date.

"Well, we better get to the airport then, da?"

There would be no second chances. As soon as Astrid left Haiti she would become a ghost. They had no other leads, no other way of finding her. Unless they made it to the airport, every sacrifice they had made, every life lost would be for nothing. Bishop wouldn't allow the deaths to go unpunished. They would make it. They had to.

Bishop hobbled, his leg still smarting. As they rounded the corner of the police vehicle, Bishop's face folded into confusion.

"Ah, Oleg? Where's your car?"

Oleg scoffed. "It's over…" His head darted around, perplexed. "It was right here!"

"Oleg, did you leave the keys in the car?"

"Yes, but…"

"It's probably already parts, my friend. Most lawless place on earth, right?"

"Пиздец, Жопа, ебать, сука!"

"We can't stay here, Oleg."

"Da." He composed himself. "Can you walk? We can head back to the dock."

"I can walk, but we're not heading to the dock."

"What?" The realisation was slapped across his face. "No. Are you insane? We can't! We won't make it in time."

The MI6 agent shrugged. "They took the long way. We know a shortcut."

Bishop glanced towards Cité Soleil. A population of four hundred thousand with no government presence, embedded crime and armed violence.

Limping towards the driver's side of the van, Bishop yanked the door open. Astrid's militia hadn't had time to strip the bodies of weapons. They both had a sidearm which Bishop pocketed. The radio had been shot out and was a sparking mess. Feeling nauseous, he sat on the bullet-riddled front bumper.

"You *are* insane." Oleg eyes were wide with amazement. "Cité Soleil is known as the most dangerous place on the planet. It would be like... like..."

"Storming hell itself?"

"Yes. Exactly that."

"Basically Dante's Inferno." Bishop nodded. "And if it means getting to Astrid, then yes, I'll do whatever it takes."

"We have no backup. Few weapons. No support. You're a mess and we only have thirty minutes to traverse through the most hazardous location on earth."

"Sounds like fun, doesn't it? You in?"

Oleg sighed, slung the submachinegun over his shoulder and extended a hand to Bishop. "Come on then, let's not keep the devil waiting. Time to storm the gates of hell."

For several minutes, they hobbled down the winding

streets of Cité Soleil unhindered. The houses, if they could be called that, were comprised of cement blocks with a metal roof. Most appeared to be made of scavenged material. There were no cars, at least none visible, nothing to provide them with a fast escape. Some of the dwellings were decorated with sick-looking plants, and there was the occasional basic shop selling sodas and cigarettes.

Residents were scattered around the streets, lounging on makeshift steps or battered plastic seats. They eyed the strangers warily, but none made aggressive moves. That may have been due to the prominent weapons they carried. The spies soon had a curious entourage following them, comprised mainly of young boys. It was perhaps the first time these people had seen a white face in the flesh. They may have been hanging around to see their first white person lynched.

Bishop recalled an article he'd read on the flight over. Someone had called Cité Soleil the microcosm of all the ills in Haitian society: endemic unemployment, illiteracy, non-existent public services, unsanitary conditions, unchecked crime and rampaging warlords. Given a choice, they hoped to avoid the last two.

Every corner, every window held potential menace. Bishop gripped his pistols tight, seeing every shadow and doorway as a threat. They walked as fast as Bishop's injuries allowed, but it seemed the neighbourhood had been alerted to their presence and everyone was waiting for the inevitable confrontation. Warlords ruled certain parts of the neighbourhood with iron fists. It was inevitable they would cross paths with one soon. When they did, Bishop hoped to reason with them. If that failed, he'd attempt to bribe them with the few hundred dollars he had in his pocket. They had to get to the airport in time.

That's if they weren't shot first. Bishop had been shot enough for one day.

He was amazed Astrid hadn't killed him when she had the chance. He doubted it was a repayment for saving her life. She didn't seem like the sentimental type. So then why? Was it true she actually cared for him? Even a tiny, insignificant amount? It was possible, though Bishop doubted it. It seemed more likely that she regretted sparing his life, if only temporarily. Given his course to the airport, it was unlikely he would last the next hour.

Regardless of whatever complicated feelings Bishop had for Astrid, he had to take her down. The woman had to face justice for her crimes. The murders, the immeasurable blood on her hands, not to mention the manipulation on a global scale. She was a sadistic arms dealer and a danger to the stability of the world. Bishop had to become a blunt instrument to capture her and to make her pay.

Distracted from his thoughts, Bishop saw a ripple of excitement flow through the residents of Cité Soleil. Something was happening. The crowd grew in both size and volume. Angry shouts were hurled in their direction. Brave young men dashed towards them, only to retreat when they got too close. They were becoming bolder, more unruly.

Oleg and Bishop sped up. It was becoming more dangerous by the second. As they walked past an old woman on a rocking chair, she pointed at them and cackled loudly.

Bishop slowed and asked, "What's so funny?"

She nodded towards a decrepit radio held together with sticky tape and hope. "You, *ya anndan chou pouri.* Da radio. Everyone here listens to da radio, in case da cops are stupid enough to try and hassle us again." The accent was heavily Creole. She blinked several times, as if distracted by a thought. She turned to them, seemingly surprised they were still there. "Dere was an announcement. Be on de lookout for two white men, one pretty badly shot up." She threw a crooked finger in Bishop's direction. "There be a reward, a bounty on your head, *kochon*. Bring da men in, dead or alive and you gets five million American dollars cash." She cackled again. "You in deep poupu, yessir! If I was twenty years younger I'd have already shot your arses, *chen sal*. You is both dead men, you just ain't buried yet. Ha!"

Oleg turned to Bishop, then to the growing crowd. "Good to see the Saudi cash being put to good use, then. Why would she do that?"

Bishop frowned. "Ah, that may have been my fault."

Slowly, Oleg turned to him. "Why?" His word was a slab of ice.

"I did suggest she could perhaps make my position more difficult."

Oleg's eyes were wide. "Why would you do that? Why would you taunt her? What is it between you two?"

It was a good question, but one for another time. Right now they had more pressing matters.

They turned to see the mounting crowd draw ever closer. The mob carried baseball bats, planks of wood, steel pipes. They were angry and hungry. A lethal combination.

Astrid had just weaponised an entire impoverished neighbourhood. She'd turned the population of Cité Soleil into assassins.

CHAPTER FIFTEEN

"Which hundred do you want?" Bishop swept his two pistols at the crowd.

Oleg unslung his submachinegun. "I'll take all the ones under four foot. The rest are yours."

"You spoil me."

"Any plans coming to mind, Englishman?"

A brick was thrown in their direction, but it went wide and smashed through the old woman's front window. The crash turned heads, but Bishop and Oleg's focus remained on the crowd in front of them.

The old woman rose from her rickety chair. "Who was dat? You gonna fix dat window. Get *manman ou*!"

"Plans?" Bishop asked as he shook his head at an encroaching kid, no older than twelve. The youth wisely backed away, staring wide-eyed at the pistol aimed in his direction. "Fire into the air. They'll scatter and we make a break for that small gap over to the right, the green fence —you see it?"

Oleg sneered. "Into the air?"

"These people are hungry and poor, Oleg. They've

been given an opportunity that comes once in five life-times. It's not their fault."

"Your affinity with the common man will get us killed, you know that?"

"You may be right." Bishop pulled back the hammer of his pistol to discourage a couple of skinny toothless men from rushing him on the side. "But we minimise losses, alright?"

"That's not a plan," Oleg replied, stony faced.

The crowd grew unruly. They had seconds before they were rushed and overpowered.

"Fine, it's not a plan." Bishop didn't wait for a response. "On three. Two."

The throaty *thrum* of a powerful engine drowned out the noise of the crowd. Many scattered at the sound, terri-fied. The remainder parted like the Red Sea. From around a corner, a huge black pick-up spewing clouds of black smoke pushed its way into the sea of bodies. The massive vehicle seemed to have been a Ford at one stage, but had been heavily modified. A white skull was hand-painted on the hood. An M60 machine gun had been welded to the roof, attached to a homemade swivel mechanism. Skulls—whether real or not Bishop couldn't tell—spears and other intimidating paraphernalia were strapped to its surface. The pick-up could have driven straight off the set of a post-apocalyptic movie.

The local warlord had arrived.

A heavy hatch on the top of the vehicle's cabin was flung open. Emerging from within was a man, no older than early twenties, wearing a white Nike t-shirt, gold chains and sporting a mohawk more suited to an eighties music video. Someone was a big *Mad Max* fan.

The warlord pulled out a baseball bat studded with nails and addressed the crowd loudly. In French, he screamed, "Nobody touch dese men! You hear? Nobody! Dey get hurt, you get hurt worse, yeah?"

Oleg glanced at Bishop hopefully.

The MI6 agent frowned. "I don't think we're better off."

The warlord leapt to the ground. Strapped to each leg were mismatching guns: a Colt 45 and a 357 Magnum. Swinging the baseball bat casually, he leered at them. He was missing several teeth, and those remaining were more crooked than an Alabama politician. Eying the spies, he smiled, but there was no humour in his eyes.

At least he spoke French. Bishop knew no Creole.

"You da men I heard about on the radio? Oohhoo!" He spun on the spot, excited. "I is Lord Jules, Esquire. At your service." The warlord assessed Bishop, lingering on the various bandages, cuts and bruises. "You in da wars, mon. You look more banged up dan da neighbourhood whore. How you still standin'?"

"Sheer force of will."

That amused Lord Jules. A genuine smile creased his features. "What you doin' in Soleil, my friends?"

"We're just passing through. We need to get to the airport urgently." Bishop gripped the pistols tighter.

Nodding sympathetically, Lord Jules scratched the underside of his chin with the bat. "Hmmm, hmmm, urgently, yessir. Ain't nobody with brains be usin' da Soleil as a shortcut, eh? Not lest dey got shit for brains, yeah?" He laughed heartily at his own joke.

"That's what I tried to tell him." Oleg thumbed in Bishop's direction. "But he refused to pay the extra taxi fare."

Lord Jules placed both hands on his back and let loose a full belly laugh. "That is funny. You is a funny man. I like you. Tell you what, mon, you both come wit' me, I give you a ride to da airport, hmmm?"

Bishop eyed Lord Jules' men as they made their way through the crowd, circling behind them. "What if we don't want to go? It's a lovely day for a walk."

"Yes, yes, it is that, yes. But I tell you sometin' friend to friend, yeah?" Lord Jules leaned in close. "You don' come wit' us, you be dead in t'ree minute." He held up three fingers to emphasise the point. "I guarantee it."

"You've got guns. We've got guns. Looks like a lot of innocent people could get hurt."

Lord Jules frowned and nodded as if conceding the point. In a smooth motion he extracted the Colt 45 and fired backwards into the crowd without looking. A young male dropped to the ground, crying in agony, clutching his wrist.

Flashing a toothless grin, Lord Jules eyed them both carefully. "Yessum. You was saying sometin' about people gettin' hurt?"

"I can make you a rich man." Bishop eyed Lord Jules's men edging closer.

"You got five million dollars on you now, hmm?"

"No, but I can—"

"Oh, dat a shame, a real shame." He shook his head, but made sure his eyes never left Bishop. "Because dere a lady who will give me five million dollars in cash today." Lord Jules said the figure with reverence. "You got dat much cash on you, hmm?"

"It's in my other trousers."

"Den it a shame you don' have dem trousers on now, eh?"

Lord Jules's men were mere feet away now, wielding machetes.

"It doesn't have to go down like this. We can discuss it like gentlemen."

"Gentlemen? Ha!" He laughed and turned to the crowd, who soon joined him, either finding it amusing or terrified of the warlord. "You call me a gentleman? Nobody ever done dat. You know why dey never do that, Mr Fancy? Do you?"

Bishop stayed silent.

"Because I took everyt'ing myself, I never ask nice." He tilted his head menacingly. "Like now." He raised the Colt to Bishop's eyeline. "Dead or alive, dey said. What you want, Mr Fancy?"

Bishop squared his jaw. "Dead."

Lord Jules regarded him quizzically. He retracted the gun and rolled the Colt around his ear. "You one crazy son of a—"

Before he could finish the sentence, Bishop drew his weapon and shot Lord Jules between the eyes, the back of his head blown away. Ducking low, Bishop took out the three of his men nearby, all clean head shots. Oleg fired the machine gun above the mob.

The crowd reacted with pandemonium. Some dropped to the ground. Most scattered to the periphery. Others saw it as an opportunity to rush the foreigners. Three of those carrying makeshift weapons were cut down in quick succession by the spies. Others, having seen their comrades expurgated so brutally and efficiently, backed away, but they didn't leave.

Bishop broke into a run towards the pick-up. "Change of plan."

Running to catch up, Oleg replied, "You didn't have a plan to begin with!"

The young man on the back of the pick-up swivelled the M60 machine gun their way. Bishop picked him off with a bullet through the brain. Another poked out of the vehicle's cabin, struggling to pull out a rusted six shooter. He swiftly had his head annihilated by Oleg's submachinegun.

Bishop leapt up and yanked at the door. It was welded shut. He clambered on top and jumped in, pushing off the body that was slumped across the roof. Outside, the crowd was regrouping, coming to terms with what had happened.

Oleg manned the M60 but quickly abandoned it to join Bishop. "Pure show. Empty."

It would only be moments before the crowd launched a counteroffensive.

Bishop started the hefty engine. "Want to get out of here?"

"I was hoping to stay for dinner, but if you insist."

"I do." Bishop threw the car in gear. "I really do."

The pick-up was strafed with gunfire as it churned dirt and sped away. The driver's side window shattered and bullets peppered the bodywork. Within seconds they had turned a corner and were out of the line of sight.

That didn't mean they were safe. Not by a long shot.

Navigating the narrow, unplanned streets, Bishop drove as fast as he could. On a brief straight stretch, he touched his side. His hand came back bloody.

"Son of a bitch." Bishop held his side to stem the bleeding. It was only a nick, but it hurt like hell.

"Are you a bullet magnet, man?" Oleg's face was astonished. "Do you know how many times I've taken a bullet on this mission?"

Bishop squinted, concentrating on the chaotic configuration of the streets. "I don't know, seven?"

"Not once! Look at me." Oleg swivelled his body, displaying it. "I haven't even been stabbed. Not a mark on me. But you've been shot up worse than a Moldovan road sign."

"Bully for you."

Teeth clenched, Bishop sped towards the Toussaint

Louverture International Airport. He had no idea how much time they'd lost confronting the crowd, but thanks to the pick-up they were making it back quickly. He was too jaded by the last few weeks to believe that even that minimal luck would hold, though.

A metallic knocking came from the front of the vehicle, coupled with a shuddering of the steering wheel. Pungent black smoke seeped from either side of the hood. The engine coughed and spluttered, and lost momentum.

With a palm striking the wheel, Bishop let loose a livid cry. "Once, just fucking once I'd like to catch a break on this cock-sucking mission!"

Oleg stared at him and held up his submachinegun. "Is now a good time to mention I'm out of bullets?"

The pick-up juddered and gave a fatal-sounding clanging wheeze. The engine stopped completely and the vehicle slowed, then came to an inglorious halt in front of a makeshift bar. The only thing to differentiate it from any other dwelling was the word "Bar" written in faded white paint on the front door. That and the ten hard-looking men who milled about out the front holding beer bottles.

When Oleg and Bishop climbed out of the dead vehicle the group of locals took intense interest in the two white men. Many wore cheerful expressions, as if someone had just handed them five million dollars.

Oleg sniffed and stared them down, empty machine gun in hand. "Can you run?"

"I don't think we'll outrun this lot." They all appeared relatively fit, Bishop thought.

"Oh, I don't have to outrun them. I just have to outrun you."

"Charming."

Oleg aimed the useless weapon warningly at a particularly bold local wearing a Tupac t-shirt. To Bishop he said, "You should try negotiating with them. It worked so well last time."

"I was doing alright there for a while."

"Until you shot the warlord in the face."

"Well, yes, apart from the whole face shooting thing, I'd categorise the negotiations as quite promising."

The two spies eyed the ten men. The upside was that they were unarmed. The downside was that they couldn't be outrun, at least not in Bishop's condition. In his present state he'd be hard pressed to outrun a pot plant.

Leaning against Oleg, Bishop aimed the two pistols at the men. He spoke French. "Anything I can help you gentlemen with?"

A few watched, confused, as most of the population only spoke Creole. The lead man, bald and with a neck like a truck tyre, frowned. "We good here, man." His French was heavily accented, but understandable. "We good. You havin' problems wit' your car dere?"

Bishop glanced back at the smoking, bullet-ridden vehicle. "No, why do you ask?"

The bald man nodded and rubbed the stubble on his chin. "Dat looks like Lord Jules's car. He not stupid enough to drivin' up in here. No sir. He do, an' he gonna get awful dead I t'ink."

"I don't believe he's going to be overly concerned by that any longer."

A youth, perhaps ten, sprinted away, racing out of sight like a sewer rat, no doubt to alert the local warlord that all their collective Christmases had arrived. Perhaps the men were less of a threat in the short term. Their job was probably to distract the two until the real muscle arrived. If that was the case, Oleg and Bishop had minutes at best.

"I'll lay down supressing fire and we hustle down the lane, the one on the left."

"Excellent." Oleg nodded. "And where will you obtain the wheelchair from?"

"I can make that distance, I assure you."

"No doubt, but we can't afford to wait the week it would take."

"Debate is over." Bishop turned and aimed his two pistols at the approaching men. They backed away, holding hands in the air. None ran, as if waiting for an opportunity. "On three."

Oleg raised an eyebrow and nodded at the two guns in Bishop's hands. "Can I have one of those?"

"No. You were snippy. Snippy people don't get guns. Two."

"You're an idiot."

In the distance the low rumble of an engine told them another warlord was en route. Given their recent history with warlords, Bishop was keen to be anywhere but the most dangerous place on earth facing down a murderous sociopath. He was fussy like that.

"One."

Bishop fired into the air and the men scattered. A few were foolish enough to stand their ground, but he aimed at their feet and the bottles on the makeshift table and they dove for cover or ran for the hills.

The two spies ran. The pain ripped through Bishop like spears. Every limb felt like it was being wrenched from his body. The agony almost made him black out, but he stayed the course, limping to their rendezvous point free of pursuers. Though it wouldn't be long before they were flushed out of the labyrinth by the newly appointed assassins.

Gasping, Bishop said, "Told you I'd make it."

"You probably left a trail of blood."

"I didn't," Bishop replied indignantly before checking. He hadn't.

The spot they had found was a tiny alcove between buildings. A rusted tin roof offered shade from the afternoon sun. It was shielded from view from either end of the street, but anyone searching thoroughly would find them soon enough. They were too exposed. They were staving off the inevitable and they both knew it.

For the life of him, Bishop couldn't recall the last time he'd smiled. The all-encompassing torture of this mission had multiplied until only pain remained. Perhaps another day he'd smile again, but it seemed unlikely. He had to survive this one first.

Bishop handed one pistol to Oleg while he checked the other. Bishop's was empty. The SRV agent checked his; only a few bullets remained. They exchanged despondent expressions. The big Russian poked his head out in search of angry locals.

There was no way they could keep this up. Without transport they couldn't make the airport in time. In Bishop's condition, they'd be lucky to make the next block.

They had no support. No comms. No time. A whole city out to kill them. And they were virtually out of bullets. Bishop had been in tough positions before and had always managed to fight his way out, but he couldn't recall anything quite this grim and hopeless.

Oleg rose to one knee. "Well, I would like to say it has been a pleasure," he offered his hand, "but we know this would be a lie."

Bishop blinked several times. "You're leaving?"

"Have you not been paying attention? Hundreds of thousands of impoverished people have been offered a chance to escape their unfortunate lives. Take a look at yourself. That chance is you, my friend. If you last beyond the end of this sentence I will be surprised." Oleg raised both eyebrows, waited a couple of seconds, then frowned. "I am surprised." He handed Bishop the empty machine gun. "Here, perhaps this will stave off death for a few seconds."

"At least give me the loaded weapon; even the odds?"

With a frown, Oleg seemed to contemplate the idea. "No. You were snippy. I will keep this."

"You bastard." Snatching the empty weapon, Bishop tossed it aside and stared at the Russian. "You're letting Astrid get away!"

"Did I say this?" He shook his head. "I said I was leaving you. I am still on my mission. I am SVR. I will complete my assignment. I can only do this without a dead man dragging me down. Farewell. I hope you die quickly."

Bishop clenched his teeth. "I wish you the same."

Without another word, Oleg stood, checked the narrow road and sprinted into the light. He didn't look back.

Fucker.

How could he leave Bishop? Surely he realised he was signing his death warrant? Bishop knew they weren't friends, but even so, the defection was cold-blooded. Oleg had literally left him for dead. If by some miracle Bishop survived, he vowed revenge on the treacherous Russian. After Astrid, of course.

Lots of revenge.

The battered MI6 agent took a deep breath and gazed at the two empty weapons in his hands. There were a million obstacles between Bishop and his prey. He could hardly walk. It would be all too easy to lie down and die. Very easy. But that wasn't how Bishop was wired. There was too much fight in him, always had been. Unsteadily, he pushed himself up. He was bloody, he was bruised and unlikely to make it more than a hundred metres. But he had to try. There was no other choice.

Bishop took a shaky step into the light, preparing to take on an entire city, alone.

CHAPTER SIXTEEN

Limping, Bishop eyed the darkened doorways and windows of Cité Soleil. Faces looked out at him. Some were curious, some angry, others had hungry expressions. No one came out or even spoke to him.

Bishop knew it wouldn't hold. There were five million reasons it wouldn't. He hobbled on regardless. Whether it was stubbornness, a quest for retribution or complete stupidity, he could no longer tell. He was too spent. Already a mess from his previous injuries, the addition of the new gunshot wound sapped his strength. His feet dragged, carving lines in the dirt. Only memory kept him moving now, but that too would be exhausted soon enough.

Behind him, Bishop heard urgent whispers and tentative footsteps. He turned to see five youths, four boys and a girl following him at a distance. Their expressions were more than idle curiosity, they shone brightly with anticipation. The four boys were handsome and confident, with straight backs and strong strides. The girl hung back, holding one arm across herself defensively, head down, hair half covering her face. It was the stance of someone who had been beaten down by life already.

They saw that Bishop had noticed them and seemed emboldened by this. They quickened their pace and closed the gap. In no condition to outrun them, the MI6 agent slowed to a halt, unsure if he would be able to summon the energy to move again. He stared at the group, awaiting their move. They tried to conceal various machetes and knives behind their backs. The smallest comically did his best to hide a baseball bat.

Tired, Bishop grunted, "Go away."

A short stocky boy yelled, "Make us!" before retreating to the back of the pack.

Bishop waved the guns in their general direction in some sort of vague threat, then turned and trod onward. His little gang of admirers drew closer.

The tallest of them, wearing a porter's uniform from a local hotel, stepped in front. In English, he said, "I'm tinkin' if you had bullets in dem guns you woulda fired dem already, cha? But you ain't."

"An astute observation." Bishop paused and casually aimed one in his direction. "Probably."

The youth grinned a broad, white-toothed grin. "Nah, man, I t'ink you got nothin' in dem bangers, yeah."

"That so?" Bishop tilted his head. "Willing to bet your life on it?"

"Mebe." He stepped forward. His words were brave, but there was real fear in his eyes. He flicked his fingers, gesturing for his friends to circle either side of Bishop.

"So whacha gonna do, Mister?" He grew more emboldened by the second. "You fire one shot in da air and we skip, yeah? Just one. Promise." He beamed. "Dat is, unless you empty like my sister's belly?"

The pistol and the machine gun felt heavy in his hands. Bishop exhaled a heavy sigh. There was no longer a need for pretence. The jig was up. He let go and they clattered to the ground.

Startled, the girl ran off. Whether it was in fear or to gather others, Bishop didn't care. He didn't want her to be around for what was to come. He was sure she had seen her share of death already.

Exhausted, Bishop raised his fists. The youths laughed. They moved within a step of him.

"You ka hardly stand, mon!" The tallest youth looked around for his friends to join him in his revelry. "How you gonna fight us four, eh? Tough man? You answer me dat!"

"Like this."

The first punch landed squarely on the tall youth's nose. Staggering backwards, he clutched at his broken nose, a cascade of blood already flooding down his face. A second youth heaved a machete at Bishop's upper body. The move was so telegraphed, Bishop had time to react and have a cup of tea if he wanted. Dropping to his knee, he delivered a series of rib-cracking body blows.

With no idea where these last vestiges of energy reserves had come from, Bishop knew he had seconds left before he collapsed, completely spent. The third boy came at him with a knife, blade down, slashing as he approached. Using footwork to circle in a tiny dance with his attacker, Bishop kept his eye on the blade. When the strike came, it was clumsy and uncommitted. The trained MI6 agent grasped his wrist, used the momentum to aid his twist and promptly broke the kid's wrist at the joint.

With an unbelievably painful sting, Bishop's head rang like a bell and he staggered sideways. His vision blazed white, fuzzy around the edges. The blow from the baseball bat had been delivered expertly. Bishop had collected a full swing that would have felled most people, but he was too obstinate for that. Rounding on the kid,

Bishop shook his head to rid himself of the pain. Buoyed by his initial success, the youth went in for another hit. But this time Bishop was ready.

The strike was a direct blow. Bishop swerved under it, using his upper arm to glance the blow harmlessly away. He didn't want to hurt the kid, but the anger had welled too much. Using all the might he had left, he punched the youth square in the jaw. If he were at full capacity, the blow would have broken his jawbone. As it was, the kid would have a nasty bruise for a week or so. He stumbled backwards, clutching his jaw, screaming.

All four attackers subdued, at least in the short term, Bishop slumped forward, the full force of his exhaustion bearing down on him. He had nothing left. He was done. Vision blurring, he attempted to stagger away, but tripped on a writhing body on the ground. So shattered he couldn't raise his hands to protect his head, Bishop's face hit the dirt with a thud.

Blackness invaded his vision, the peripheries grew darker. He clawed at the ground, trying to crawl, to make it anywhere but where he'd fallen.

There were shouts and screams, a cacophony of noises, though he couldn't determine where from. He felt hands on him and tried weakly to brush them off, but he was too exhausted. He knew the end had arrived and there was nothing he could do.

His body was being dragged.

Everything went black.

Bishop woke with a start.

Eyes wide open, everything was still dark. For an instant, he thought the blow to his head had sent him blind, but after a few moments he realised he was in a dimly lit room. Outside was commotion; inside was calm and still.

"Don' move."

It was a woman's voice, soothing. Bishop's gaze was drawn towards the window of the tiny room. A woman sat on a battered crate, watching what he assumed was the street. She was young, early twenties. Her finely curled hair was short, framing her elegant face.

"You dragged me from the street?" Bishop coughed up blood.

"I did, ta save your fool ass. Keep yer mout' shut if ya want ta stay safe."

"Thank you."

She nodded in reply.

"English. You speak English?"

Eyes still on the fracas on the street, she replied, "Yes, we not savages here. We got schools, not government ones, but we educate ourselves. Dat because nobody else will."

Even though she eyed him intently, the woman had a lovely, kind face.

"What da hell was you t'inkin' being out dere in broad daylight, ya damn fool? You was gonna die on da street. Dat be sure."

She was feisty. Bishop liked her.

"Thank you again." Bishop flexed his hands to encourage circulation. "Are you going to hand me in?"

With a huff, she nodded towards the street. Bishop shuffled over and looked out through a crack in the curtain.

"Out dere, people are goin' crazy lookin' for you an' yer mate. Dey sell dere own granma for dat money, dat much for sure."

Outside on the street dozens of locals milled about. Some

shouted, some darted in different directions, some were just there to witness the chaotic spectacle. The tall youth in the porter's uniform who Bishop had taken out was bellowing orders. None glanced towards the tiny shack Bishop was in.

"That didn't answer my question."

Light shone on half her face. She issued Bishop with a sarcastic expression and rolled her eyes. Bishop really liked her.

"My name is Roseline. I don' have much to fix you up, Mister, but I'll try. I don' think da proper hospital would have enough, ta be hones'."

"Bishop."

Through the dirty curtains, he watched the street. Roseline used some offcuts as a tourniquet, gave him water and bread. After five minutes the commotion began to die down.

"They're about to disperse. That tall lad, the one in uniform, seems to hold some authority. I believe he's organising teams to search the streets. He's smart. He's just looking in the wrong direction."

Roseline squeezed past Bishop, her soft skin brushing against his. "You observant. Dat Jacob. He's a good boy, jus' easily led."

As the crowd dispersed, finally leaving the street close to deserted, Bishop allowed himself to slightly relax. He knew he was far from safety. Roseline finished tending to Bishop's wounds. Her hands were not as delicate as her features, but she seemed to know at least some basic first aid.

"W'at you doin' in Cité Soleil?"

"I'm here by accident, I assure you. I was on my way to the Hemingway Bar at the Ritz Paris and seem to have gotten a bit lost."

"Yeah, you t'ink you funny, but you ain' all that."

"So I've been told. I'm sorry to have troubled you. I do appreciate your help."

Roseline nodded. "No good ever come from white men 'ere. White men 'ave always made promises and never turned out good. I was at a football match in 2005 put on by da white man. Meant to be for peace, dey said. Dat day ended in bloodshed when da police officers shoot up da stadium, and gangs wit' machetes hacked up da fleeing spectators." Her eyes bore into him. "Then I seen the blue hats of the UN, the peace-keepers you call them, shoot men, women, in the head. That is not peace, Mister. Not even where I come from."

"Then why help me?"

"Because hate don' stop hate. Same way bullet don' stop bullet. Gandhi said you haveta break the cycle of violence."

"I fear you're far wiser than I, Roseline."

"Prolly." She winked. "Either way, I have ta get you out o' here. Dey might start looki' in da houses soon."

"Any ideas?"

"Jus' one."

"One will do." Bishop tilted his head towards the woman who had saved his life. "I'll tell you what, Rose-line of Cité Soleil. If I survive this, I'll buy you dinner. The fanciest dinner you could possibly imagine."

She squinted and didn't speak for several moments. "I'd like dat, the dinner. You actually mean dat, don' you? I read people good. You mean what you say."

"Almost always."

"Good enough." Her teeth shone. "Den again, could be da pain talkin'. You lost a lotta blood. You delirious. You stay here."

"You're leaving me?"

"Ha, if I was gonna claim da money I woulda

screamed down da walls by now. But I ain't, okay? You stay, I be back before you can say Wyclef Jean."

Before Bishop could protest further, Roseline was out the door. The woman held his fate in her hands. She could claim the prize for herself, but he didn't think she would. It could have been the delirium speaking, but Bishop believed she was acting in his best interests.

In what seemed like hours, but was likely only minutes, Roseline returned. In her hand was a large battered motorbike helmet. She threw it at him.

"Put it on. You goin' for a ride."

Knowing his time was limited, he did exactly as she requested. Unsteady on his feet, Bishop pushed through the pain and stepped onto the street, helmet on. A kid, seemingly no older than twelve, sat atop an idling beaten-up motorbike, held together by makeshift welds and electrical tape.

"Who's that?" Bishop's voice was muffled under the visor.

"He my cousin, ya. He can be trusted."

"How do you know?"

"Because if he don' do what I say," she raised her voice towards her cousin, "I gonna slap him upside o' de head so hard."

"Hardly reassuring."

"You in da wrong part of the world for reassuring, Mr Bishop. Now, is you ready?"

"Not even a little."

She looked down at the white skin of his hands. "Not much we can do dere." She shrugged. "Good luck." She slapped him hard on the back. "You gonna need it." Pointing to the bike, Roseline said, "Get on den."

Not needing to be asked twice, Bishop threw a leg over the bike, holding the thin frame of Roseline's cousin. The boy was even slighter than he appeared.

"Where to?" she asked.

"The airport, international departures, please. And fast."

Roseline chortled. "Fast is all he know."

After exchanging a few urgent Creole words with Roseline, the kid dropped the bike into gear, twisted his wrist and the bike flew off. Bishop held on for dear life and didn't have time to glance back at the woman who had saved him.

The kid was either a motocross professional in training or suicidal. Possibly both. The youth wove through the unruly neighbourhood with ease, never slowing. Bishop clung tightly to his slight frame. Along the dirty streets, through infinitesimally tight gaps where there didn't seem to be a road at all, the motorbike powered on. Roseline's cousin sped through it all at breakneck speed.

Bishop had to wonder why his exposed white hands had been a problem at all. They were travelling at such a speed they would be nothing but a blur. Finding it hard to stay focused, Bishop watched the world weave by. It was claustrophobic and hectic, and then suddenly it wasn't.

In an instant, the confined space of Cité Soleil gave way to an open field with freshly mown grass behind a chain-link fence. Threading the bike through a gap, the kid sped into the grounds of the Toussaint Louverture International Airport.

In the space of a few short minutes Bishop had gone from certain death to being within reach of his goal. He checked his watch. They were cutting it fine, but there was still a chance.

The head of Kali was within his grasp once more.

CHAPTER SEVENTEEN

The executive lounge of the Toussaint Louverture Airport was much like any other the world over. Perhaps a little smaller and slightly more weathered than some, but it seemed to offer the same amenities as most.

Bishop wasn't interested in amenities.

The immaculately dressed woman at the front desk certainly seemed to fit the mould. Prim, with hair tied back so tightly it could have created its own black hole, her make-up was thick but perfectly applied. As Bishop's bloodied, limping form hobbled through the entrance to the first-class lounge she let out a shriek. Ignoring her, Bishop used his final remnants of energy to propel him to his goal.

"Sir," she huffed around the desk. "Sir, do you have a first-class ticket, sir?"

Bishop found it amusing that even in his battered and bruised state she still had the politeness to address him as sir. Ambling forward, the MI6 agent scanned the room. The only international flight out that afternoon hadn't boarded yet. She should still be in the lounge.

"Sir, I really must insist."

Bishop swatted her away like a fly.

"I'll call the police!"

There, next to the window. Astrid sat alone, absent-mindedly swirling a straw in a cocktail, unaware of the commotion at the front desk.

Bishop turned to the irritated receptionist. "As you like."

She scuttled away in a bluster. Paying her no mind, Bishop limped forward. The head of Kali was alone, reclining on a couch, no henchmen in sight. Astrid must have assumed that once she was through security she was safe. Not that her security team could bring weapons to protect her anyway.

Staggering the final few steps, Bishop issued a polite cough. Annoyed, Astrid turned. Once she realised who it was, her jaw dropped, as did her drink. It clattered onto the tile floor, the glass smashing into pieces.

It didn't take long before she regained her composure. "You look like absolute hell. How are you still standing? Look at you."

"Vengeance is a powerful motivator." Bishop subtly pushed his knee against the couch to prevent him from collapsing. "It's over, Astrid."

Self-control regained, she smiled amiably. "What are you going to do, bleed on me?"

"Arrest you."

"Ha! You and what army?"

"This one."

Without looking, Bishop thumbed behind him. A phalanx of Haitian police swarmed into the lounge, causing the receptionist to shriek. He could have worked with Roseline to find a phone and just call it in but he *needed* to see her go down. And not in a good way.

Bishop tilted his head. "In light of your carnage at the Port, these gentlemen would like a word."

The deaths she'd caused, the pain and suffering she'd inflicted, there was no way Bishop would miss the opportunity to see justice done. To see the expression on Astrid's face when she realised it was all at an end.

All deportment vaporised, Astrid's face turned cold, acidic. He was right. It had been worth it to see her face contort from confidence to stoniness to outright fear. She knew she'd finally reached the end of her chain, and it was he who had yanked it.

She sneered. "You've made a powerful enemy today, Bishop. I hope you know that."

As two senior police officers barged forward to handcuff her, Bishop slumped onto the couch. He clicked his fingers to garner the attention of a passing waiter.

Still watching Astrid, he sighed. "At this stage I honestly don't care." To the perplexed waiter, Bishop leaned forward. "Please grab the largest bottle of scotch you have, pour a tiny bit into a glass and bring me the remainder of the bottle. Oh, and some ice." He turned his attention back to Astrid. "If the Haitians ever give you up, you'll be facing ten lifetimes behind bars."

"My people will—"

"I don't care."

The waiter arrived with a tray, a hefty glass, a large block of ice and an ice pick. It seemed he was to perform the new trend of preparing ice in front of a customer. Bishop didn't care for it. Ice was ice. Making a song and dance out of it didn't change the fact that it was still frozen water. *Just give me the damn ice and be done with it.*

The handcuffs were secured and Astrid cast a stare as icy as anything on the tray before him.

"Swear revenge or whatever," Bishop lay back on the couch, "I'm too tired to care." He waved dismissively. "Bye bye." Turning towards the bar, he shouted, "Scotch?"

One of the police officers leaned towards Bishop. "You need urgent medical attention."

Bishop waved him away too. "Later. Later."

The scotch arrived and Bishop sat up to pour himself an exceedingly large glass, sloshing a good measure on the table in the process. Lacking the energy required to chip his own ice, he went without. He took a sip and closed his eyes.

The sound of the purveyor of his pain being led away was music to his battered ears. For a glorious few seconds he believed it would be the last thing he heard before he drifted off to sleep.

He was wrong.

The prim receptionist once again yelped, this time in a different pitch, somehow even higher than before. Reluctantly, Bishop pried his heavy eyelids open to see a heaving body burst through reception. He was unblemished by his ordeal, but flushed. Just as Bishop had, the new arrival ignored the screeching receptionist to scan the room for Astrid. He found something else.

Strolling towards Bishop, Oleg couldn't hide his astonishment. "How did you make it here so soon? I left you—"

"For dead? Yes, I do recall. I swore revenge right after you left. I really must repay that at some stage."

"I—"

"She's been arrested. The local police just took her away. They're rounding up her cohorts. No thanks to you."

Still seeming perplexed by the sudden turn of events, Oleg sat next to Bishop. "For what it's worth, I apologise for leaving you for dead."

With a Herculean effort, Bishop sat up and leaned forward. "No hard feelings."

Reaching down, Bishop grabbed the ice pick and

slammed it into Oleg's leg. Instantly blood poured from the wound. Yowling, the Russian leapt up and cradled his haemorrhaging injury. The assembled patrons of the first-class lounge, already startled, gawked at the big man hopping around, screaming Russian blue murder.

In response, the MI6 agent took a sip of scotch, reclined on the comfortable couch and closed his eyes. For the first time in what seemed like weeks, Bishop smiled.

EPILOGUE

The crowd gathered around the limousine, mesmerised. It had been several days since their neighbourhood had been rocked by the search for the two men supposedly in their midst. Since then, officials had advised that the five million dollar reward had been a hoax, and no genuine offer ever existed.

It was lucky, because once again, Bishop found himself in Cité Soleil. Several locals asked him who he was and what he was doing in their city. He gave the inquisitive locals an enigmatic grin, offering no reply.

With the use of a cane, he hobbled to the door and knocked. It took several seconds before the door flew open.

"What is it n—"

Roseline's jaw dropped. Bishop couldn't help but smile. Her shock was absolute. She obviously never expected to see the odd foreigner ever again.

"I'm here to repay my debt."

"I… what?"

"Remember? I said if I ever got out alive I'd buy you dinner." Bishop spun—albeit slowly—to demonstrate that he was indeed alive. "We have reservations at Observatoire Restaurant at eight. I'm told it's the most expensive restaurant in all of Port-au-Prince, offering stunning views of the shimmering city."

"Observatoire…" She seemed in awe. Roseline shook her head, trying to snap herself out of it. "I… I'd love to, but I don' have a t'ing to wear to such a…"

She stopped herself when Bishop held up a delicate light blue satin dress.

"It's…" She moved closer and touched the fabric. "It's beautiful." Leaning down, she checked the tag and regarded him quizzically. "It's my size."

"You mentioned I was observant, remember?" He held the dress out to her. "Shall we?"

The grin almost consumed her entire face.

Half an hour later the two were seated overlooking the lights of the city and the expanse of the bay. They sat in an exclusive corner; Bishop was assured by the maître d it was their very finest table. Bishop believed him. The view was stunning.

The vision across the table was equally pleasant. Resplendent in her new dress, Roseline was clearly enthralled by the goings-on of the restaurant.

The napkins fascinated her, as did the choice of food and drink available. She spoke to the staff as real humans, asking if they enjoyed their work, and seemed genuinely interested in their answers. Bishop relished her innocence, her appreciation of things he too often took for granted.

When the first course arrived, they toasted one another, but her face fell, as if a sense of gloom had overcome her.

Bishop put down his glass. "What's wrong?"

Her demeanour was forlorn. "I'll remember dis night forever." There was melancholy in her tone. "My one glimpse of a life I'll never have." As if only just realising she was speaking aloud, she shook her head. "I apologise. Well too sad for such a generous night."

He frowned. "I'm afraid you're under a misapprehension." Her face creased in confusion. Bishop continued. "Tonight isn't the end. It's just the beginning. That five million dollars you so selflessly declined? It's yours, compliments of His Majesty's government." He raised a glass of champagne. "Welcome to your new life, Roseline."

For Bishop, the expression of shock on the young woman's face was almost worth everything he'd been through.

THE END

Hey there,

Bishop won the day.

But is he ready for the next escapade? Are you?

Bishop returns and this time its personal – *Agent Provocateur.*

When Bishop's former mentor threatens to instigate a nuclear war, the MI6 agent dives headlong into a deeply personal mission where nothing is quite what it seems.

Racing across China with hounds snapping at his heels, Bishop is forced to confront not only a relentless adversary, but demons from his own past.

Full throttle action, snappy dialogue and twists at every turn, *Agent Provocateur* will have you turning pages late into the night.

Want to know when *Agent Provocateur* is out?

Sign up to my VIP Book Club and be the first to know: https://davesinclair.com.au/newsletter/

Thanks for reading!

Dave Sinclair

P.S. If you enjoyed the read, please consider leaving a review. It really helps a lot.

ABOUT DAVE SINCLAIR

Dave Sinclair is a novelist, a screenwriter and a really excellent parallel parker.

He lives in Melbourne, Australia with his two crazy daughters. He's also an award-winning filmmaker, a title that sounds far more impressive than it really is. He won a best comedy screenplay and cinematography award for a short film he wrote and directed, though at the time he didn't really know what cinematography was. A completed screenplay is currently doing the rounds.

Dave's overflowing bookshelves include many works by Douglas Adams, P.G. Wodehouse, Dashiell Hammett, Raymond Chandler, Janet Evanovich, Ian Fleming, Zadie Smith and John le Carré.

The Eva Destruction books are stories Dave wanted to read, full of action, laughs and fascinating characters. Eva has many more adventures up her tattooed sleeves.

To find out more, you can stalk Dave at his semi-reputable website: https://davesinclair.com.au

ACKNOWLEDGMENTS

It was kind of daunting starting a new series, but luckily the first Bishop book came together pretty seamlessly and I had a blast throwing the characters in the deep end. The next two books are locked and loaded and will be a lot of fun.

For readers of the Eva Destruction series, hopefully you had a ball finding out what makes Bishop tick.

If you're a new reader, welcome! You're in for a ride. If you haven't met Eva Destruction yet, you're most welcome to look her up. The events in the Bishop books take place before those in the Eva Destruction series, but don't worry, there's no big spoilers.

Now for the actual acknowledgements!

First and biggest thanks goes to my amazing partner, Kristi. She's my biggest cheer squad and still manages to get excited when I message her that I've finished another chapter.

Or at least pretend to get excited, let's be honest, there's a lot of chapters. Monkey heart unicorn, you're amazing.

To my girls, Esther and Quinn, their boundless energy

is an inspiration. The literary world is on notice as both have started to write their own books (so far there's plenty of unicorns and bunnies). The literary world won't be the same once the Sinclair girls are let loose.

Every writer needs a tribe. Pretty sure I've found the craziest writing tribe there is. The G-Mob are all amazing writers and even better drinkers. Craig, Justin, Luke, Nathan, Steve, Amanda and Amanda have provided support, assistance, insight and laughter when I need it most. Go read their stuff! http://genremob.com/

To my talented sis, Ali, thank you for always being so supportive. Check out her books here - http://allisinclair.com. She even dedicated her last book to me, which was amazingly sweet. I dedicated this book to the cat.

A big thank you to my editor Vanessa Lanaway. She fiixes my mystakes goud. She's also a great human. Thanks to Nathan who formats my pages to make me look almost professional.

Thanks to Amanda Pillar (a great writer you should look up) who designed all the Bishop covers. Check out her cover work here - https://www.smokinghotcovers.com/

Thanks to my beta team, Steve & Gerard. I took every suggestion onboard. Well, some. Okay, a few. Alright, that one thing about the duck. And thank you to my intrepid team of book ninjas who get to read after I've made changes.

Thank you also goes to my VIP Book Club team who receive my exclusive newsletter. One lucky newsletter reader, Corissa Palfrey won a competition to have her mum's name (Betty Jo Anne Palfrey) appear in this book so she could be killed off. That's love, people.

Reader feedback helps me along too, so don't be afraid to reach out on Facebook, Twitter, Instagram, on the street, hiding in my closet, that kind of thing. You can stalk me at all these semi-reputable places:

www.davesinclair.com.au

https://twitter.com/thedavesinclair

https://www.instagram.com/davesinclairauthor/

https://facebook.com/DaveSinclairAuthor/

Finally, thank you to the reader. I love hearing from you, and don't be shy dropping a review, it is greatly appreciated. Thank you and here's to many more adventures!

Until next time, cheers!

www.ingramcontent.com/pod-product-compliance
Lightning Source LLC
Chambersburg PA
CBHW021423110726
47901CB00008B/2274